CHRISTMAS IN THE *Country*

CHRISTMAS IN THE *Country*

Returning Home for Christmas Stirs Up Two Romances from the Past

JEANIE SMITH CASH
CHRISTINE LYNXWILER

ISBN 1-59789-341-2

Cover by Getty Images
Photographer: David Prince
Illustrations: Mari Goering

Published by Barbour Publishing, Inc., P.O. Box 719, Uhrichsville, Ohio 44683, www.barbourbooks.com

Our mission is to publish and distribute inspirational products offering exceptional value and biblical encouragement to the masses.

Printed in the United States of America.
5 4 3 2 1

A Christmas Wish

by Jeanie Smith Cash

Dedication

To Jesus, my Lord and Savior, who made this all possible. To my son, Donny; my mother, Wanda; and my brother-in-law, Marvin. You went to be with the Lord before you had a chance to read this book. Thank you for your love, support, and confidence in me as a writer. I miss you but know that I will see you again. To my own special hero, Andy. You are always there for me, and I love you. To my daughter, Robyn; son-in-law, Dave; grandchildren, Daniel, Chelsea, and Justin; my father, Don; and sister, Chere, for your love and support. To my critique partner and special friend, Barbara Warren, for your help, love, and support. A special thank-you to Kathleen Y'Barbo, Christine Lynxwiler, Janet Lee Barton, and Rebecca Germany for giving me a chance.

As for God, his way is perfect;
the word of the LORD is flawless.
He is a shield for all who take refuge in him.

PSALM 18:30 NIV

Chapter 1

Abigail Forrester ran through the airport, pulling her luggage behind her. Thankfully, she had decided to fly out of San Francisco. The way she dodged in and out of passengers on the way to her gate, people would surely think she was crazy. But she had no choice. If anything held her up, she'd miss her flight. Out of breath, with her heart pounding and a pain in her side, she rushed into the security checkpoint and dumped everything onto the conveyor belt. She said a prayer of thanks when she slid through the doorway and didn't set off the alarm. After her bags were checked, she made a mad dash for the gate and arrived just as the agent was about to close the door.

"Please wait. That's my flight!" Abby handed him her ticket, hoping that because she'd been upgraded to first class, he'd still allow her to board.

He frowned momentarily but reached to accept the coupon. "Follow me, please. I'd suggest you give yourself a little more time in the future. Another second and you would have missed this flight."

"I know, and I'm sorry. I really appreciate this; I was unavoidably detained." Heat filled Abby's cheeks as she remembered the reason she had been delayed. As manager of a travel agency in Tracy, California, a small town about fifty miles from the airport, she took pride in being organized. How could she have left her wallet locked in the drawer of her desk at work? She'd had to call Bonnie Cranston, owner of the agency, who had offered to bring the wallet to her. The hour-and-a-half wait for Bonnie to arrive had almost caused her to miss her flight.

"I'll take those for you." The flight attendant lifted her bag and placed it in the compartment above her head as Abby took her seat and sighed in relief.

"You almost didn't make it." The man's deep voice echoed from the seat next to her.

Abby froze. She'd recognize that voice anywhere. *Oh, Lord,* she prayed silently, *let me be mistaken. Please don't let it be him.* She slowly turned to look at the man beside her. She wondered which of them appeared more shocked.

"Nick?" She swallowed against a suddenly dry throat and forced her gaze to meet his. "What are you doing here?"

"I've been at a medical convention for the last two days." The dimples she remembered so well creased his lean cheeks as he smiled at her. "Do you live in San Francisco?"

"N–no," she stammered and could have kicked herself for allowing him to still affect her this way. She fastened her safety belt before answering, hoping to get a grip on her emotions. "I live about fifty miles inland."

"Jared said you'd moved away, but he didn't say where." Nick placed the magazine he'd been reading back into the seat in front of him and adjusted his medical bag to give her more room.

Oh, Lord, I know You have a reason for everything. But of all the people to find in the seat next to me, why did it have to be Nicholas Creighton?

He hadn't changed at all. His muscular six-four

frame didn't sport an ounce of fat. Eyes a brilliant shade of green, dark brown hair that barely brushed his collar, and a warm, welcoming smile that still had the power to turn her bones to liquid. How could she be so attracted to him when he'd crushed her the way he had? Even now, hurt nearly overwhelmed her at just seeing him again. The chance that she might run into him once she arrived at Granny's house had crossed her mind. But she hadn't been prepared to see him this soon.

Nick and her oldest brother, Jared, had been best friends when they were growing up, and they had gone to medical school together. Nick specialized in surgery, and Jared was a pediatrician.

"How's Janine doing?" She nearly choked just saying that name. She had spent hours on her knees the night Nick had told her he was going to marry Janine, asking the Lord to please make the other woman go away and praying that Nick would change his mind and come back to her. But that had been fourteen months ago. She hoped she'd gained some perspective since then, but considering her reaction to his unexpected presence, it didn't look hopeful.

A flash of pain appeared in Nick's eyes before he

answered, making her wonder if they might be having problems. "I'm sorry; maybe I shouldn't have asked."

"No, it's all right," he said softly and patted her hand. "You don't know do you?"

"Know what?" she asked, frowning slightly.

Nick took a deep breath before answering her. "Janine died eight months ago."

Abby gasped at his words. "I'm so sorry. I had no idea. My family didn't say a word." *Oh, Lord, when I asked You to make her go away, I didn't mean for her to die! I just meant for her to move somewhere away from Nick; I didn't want her to have him. I was jealous, but I never meant for anything to happen to her.*

Nick interrupted her prayer. "It's okay, Abby. I'm sure they were trying to protect you. I didn't exactly make points with your family after hurting you the way I did." He glanced over at her, and she could see regret reflected in his eyes.

"Jared wouldn't tell me where you were when I asked—not that I blame him." His gaze slowly scanned her face. "If you were my sister, I'd probably react the same way. He said he loved me like a brother, but you had made a new life for yourself, and he felt it was best if I stayed away from you."

An odd mixture of emotions gripped Abby. Sadness filled her heart at his loss, but she wasn't ready to forgive the hurt he'd inflicted. Still, her conscience rebelled at the way she had prayed; it wasn't okay. Ashamed, she realized she hadn't acted with a very Christian attitude. *Please forgive me, Lord.* Suddenly it dawned on her what Nick had just said. She sat up in her seat and looked at him. "You asked about me?"

"Yes." He smiled sadly, adjusting his medical bag under the seat in front of him to make more room for his feet. "After Janine died, I wanted to try to reach you to explain. I know I hurt you terribly, but there is an explanation that I couldn't give you until now."

His hopeful look almost swayed her as she looked into his too-familiar eyes and felt a stab of long lost love. But at the last second, she came to her senses, pulling her gaze from his as she reached up to turn off her air vent. "You don't owe me an explanation, Nick. What we had was in the past. We've both made separate lives for ourselves now."

The captain's voice came over the intercom, interrupting their conversation. "Please fasten your seat belts and prepare for takeoff."

The plane taxied to the end of the runway. As they began their ascent, fear swelled in Abby's chest, stealing her breath away and leaving her light-headed. She gripped the side of the seat until her knuckles turned white.

"Still don't like to fly, I see." Nick patted her hand gently. "It'll be all right."

Once the plane ascended into the air and leveled out, Abby released her death grip on the chair arm, and her heartbeat slowed down to almost normal. She knew it was crazy to be in the travel profession and be afraid to fly, but she hadn't been able to get past the fear that always welled up inside of her. Just the thought of being so high off the ground caused her to break out in a cold sweat.

"Going home to Granny Forrester's for the traditional Christmas Eve gathering, I presume." Nick relaxed in his seat and offered her a gentle smile.

"Yes, I look forward to it every year. Besides, Granny would be heartbroken if any of us were missing." She glanced away, trying to fill her thoughts with Granny and home rather than the hurtful memories the man sitting beside her brought to mind.

"Yes, she would. Jared and Amy invited Scotty and me to come for Christmas Eve. I hope it won't make you uncomfortable; they didn't want us to be alone."

Panic gripped her at the thought of spending more time in Nick's presence. How would she manage this? She had been with him for only a few minutes and already the painful memories flooded her mind. It wouldn't be easy, but she couldn't deprive him of being with his sister for the holidays. She adjusted her seat belt to give her a moment to compose herself before answering him. "I can understand Amy wanting you to be there. You should be with your sister on Christmas Eve. Who's Scotty?"

"My son."

Shock rendered her speechless for a moment. *Nick and Janine had a son together?* Her chest tightened as she fought to control emotions she'd thought she had put behind her. *Please, Lord, help me. I need to get over this, or it's going to be a very long week.*

"I—I didn't know you had a son," she stammered, avoiding eye contact. "How old is he?"

"Eight months and he's quite a little guy."

"Eight months?" Abby looked up at him. "Did Janine die in childbirth?" Abby couldn't believe she'd just asked that. She'd been so shocked, she'd just blurted out the first words that had come to mind. She searched his face, hoping she hadn't inflicted more pain with her thoughtless question.

"Yes," Nick said just as the pilot announced they were descending into the Denver airport. He smiled in her direction as if to let her know that he knew she hadn't meant to be unkind.

"I'm afraid I have some bad news, folks," the pilot announced just as they landed. "It's snowing so hard here in Denver that they've grounded us for an indefinite time. We aren't going to be flying tonight, and they can't promise anything for tomorrow."

"Oh no!" Abby jerked upright in her seat. "I can't stay here for two days. I won't make it to Granny's house in time to decorate the tree."

"I don't think we have much choice." Nick laid a hand on her arm in an effort to calm her. "They can't fly in these conditions."

"I have a choice." Abby pulled her tingling arm out from under his warm hand. She unfastened the seat belt and took her bag from the flight attendant.

"Abby, what are you planning to do?" Nick unfastened his own belt, and it clanked against the airplane wall.

His shoulder brushed hers as he stood up. It was times like this that Abby wished airplanes were larger. "I'm going to rent a car and drive." She slipped the strap over her shoulder, adjusting it to a more comfortable position as Nick reached under the seat for his medical bag.

He leaned over and said softly in her ear, "You can't drive thirteen hours in this snowstorm."

She moved her head as his warm breath tickled her ear, to avoid the intimate feeling it evoked. "Oh yes, I can." Abby said a silent prayer of thanks as the wall of people started moving toward the front of the plane. She followed, trying to put as much distance as she could between herself and Nick. Just as soon as there was an opening, she quickly headed out the door and up the long ramp.

"Abby, wait!" Nick called. "There's no way you're going to drive that far in this weather by yourself."

Chapter 2

A line had already formed at the rental car desk by the time Abby stepped up to wait her turn. She set her bag down and turned to face Nick as he came up behind her.

"Don't try to talk me out of renting a car. Whatever I have to do, I'm going to be at Granny's for Christmas Eve." She raised her chin stubbornly, crossing her arms in front of her.

Nick smiled, shaking his head and reaching into his pocket for his wallet. "I'm not going to try to talk you out of it. I'm going to go with you."

Abby's heart did a little flip at the thought of

spending thirteen hours in the car with Nick. Certainly a change from what she'd been feeling a short time ago on the plane. She'd only been with him an hour and a half, and the wall of protection she'd managed to build had already begun to crumble. She couldn't let that happen. The guy broke her heart fourteen months ago.

Abby knew in her mind that she should detest him, but her heart wasn't listening. She had to get a grip on her feelings. She could not allow herself to get involved with him again.

She thought for a minute before answering, but she couldn't come up with an excuse that would make sense. "All right. We're going to the same place, so I guess it would be foolish to rent two cars. We can split the cost."

"That's fine with me." Nick pulled his credit card out of his wallet.

The tall, dark-headed man behind the counter motioned them forward. "How can I help you?"

"We'd like to rent a four-wheel drive, please." Abby set her purse on the counter.

The man tapped a few keys on the computer. "We have a Chevy Trail Blazer available."

Abby glanced at Nick, and he nodded. "That's fine; we'll take it."

"I need the name, driver's license, and credit card of the person who will be driving." The clerk laid the contract on the counter.

"We'll both be driving," Abby said, digging in her purse for her wallet.

"You'll have to put it in one name and then pay extra for the other driver."

"That's fine." Nick handed him his credit card and driver's license.

"Hey, wait a minute," Abby protested as she continued searching for her wallet. "I planned to put it in my name with you as the extra driver."

"Abby, it's going to be a long trip," Nick said. "What difference does it make whose name it's in?"

She started to argue, but she hesitated when she heard the fatigue in his voice. He had been in a conference for the last two days. He was tired, yet he'd agreed to drive through with her in spite of that fact. "I guess it doesn't make any difference. But I'm paying my half."

"Fine. We can settle up later. Let's just get this done

so we can get on the road. It's going to take longer to drive than it would in normal weather, so the sooner we get started the better."

Nick's arm brushed Abby's as he reached for the pen, sending chills of awareness up her spine. She stepped back away from him and waited while he signed the contract.

"Okay." Nick slid his credit card back into his wallet and grabbed his bags. "We're all set. Let's go get your luggage before we pick up the Blazer."

"This is it; I didn't check anything." She slid the bag back on her shoulder and picked up her purse.

His eyes widened. "Where's your guitar? You never go anywhere without it."

"I don't play anymore." Nick's penetrating glance made her uncomfortable. She didn't want to discuss this.

"Why not?" He didn't budge, waiting for an answer.

"I just don't. Look, it's not a big deal. As you said, we need to get the car so we can get going. We have a long trip ahead of us, and right now I need to find a restroom before we go."

"The restrooms are right over there." Nick indicated

the two doors down and across from them.

"I may be a little while. I need to call my parents, and it should be a little quieter in there."

Nick nodded as he sat on a bench and laid his bags on the floor next to him. "No problem," he said, removing his cell phone from his pocket. "I'm going to call Maggie to let her know I've been delayed and see how Scotty is doing."

Abby left him there and walked to the door that said WOMEN. Tactfully ignoring a tearful young girl sitting alone on a bench, she walked to the other side of the expansive room and pulled out her cell phone. After a couple of rings, her father answered.

"Hi, Daddy."

She heard the concern in her father's voice as he answered. "Hi, sweetheart. Are you all right? Where are you? Your mother and I have been worried."

"I'm fine, but we're grounded in Denver, and they don't know for how long. So we've rented an SUV, and we're going to drive." She freshened her makeup at the sink while she talked to her father.

"Abby, I don't think that's a good idea. You're going to be driving in snow and nasty weather all the way through. It's snowing here, too."

"We'll be all right, Daddy. We have to get there so I can help hang the ornaments on Granny's tree, and I'm not missing the Christmas Eve gathering. This is the only way, but we'll be careful. I promise."

"You've said 'we' several times now. Surely you aren't traveling with someone you just met. I've taught you better than that."

The sternness in her father's voice brought a smile to her lips. "No, Daddy. I know him very well. Amazingly enough, Nick Creighton happened to be in San Francisco for a medical convention, and we wound up on the same plane. He's driving through with me."

Her father's silence spoke volumes.

"Daddy, I know how you feel about the way Nick treated me, but that was a long time ago. We're just two people who need to get to the same place," Abby said as she placed her makeup back into her purse.

"You be careful. Remember how devastated you were the last time."

"I know, Daddy, but I'm not going to allow that to happen, so you don't need to worry."

"Well, I do worry. I like Nick. I always have. But

after the way he hurt you, I don't want you involved with him." He paused. "I have to admit, though, being with Nick is preferable to you driving through alone."

Abby hung up the phone with a promise to call again soon and headed past the young girl who still sat in the same place on the bench. Something about her tugged on Abby's heartstrings, and she hesitated.

Lord, if You want me to talk to this girl, please give me the words to say. Abby sat down on the bench beside the young woman.

"Hi. My name is Abby. Is there anything I can do to help?" The young girl glanced up, and the desolation Abby saw in her expression wrenched her own heart.

The girl studied Abby for a moment and shook her head. "No one can help."

Abby laid her hand on the young girl's arm in a comforting manner. "Sometimes it helps to talk to someone. Why don't you start by telling me your name?"

The girl sobbed. "My name is Sandy, and I don't know what to do. I brought my boyfriend to the airport. I thought he just planned to go home to visit his parents. But before he boarded the plane, he told me he wouldn't be coming back." More tears rolled down her face.

"Well, no wonder you're upset." Abby went to the sink and wet a paper towel. She returned and handed it to Sandy.

"I just found out a week ago that I'm six weeks pregnant." Her slender shoulders shook as she cried. "Can you believe he said he'd send me the money for an abortion, but he wouldn't marry me because he doesn't love me?" She wiped her face with the towel Abby had given her.

How did this little girl get hooked up with the wrong guy at such a young age? She looked like she should still be home playing with paper dolls, not sitting in an airport bathroom pregnant and alone. *Lord, please comfort her.*

Sandy folded the paper towel in her hand. "I could never destroy my baby. I already love it. I want to be a good mother but I'm scared." She looked up, and her tear-filled eyes begged Abby to understand.

"You love your child, Sandy, so that's a step in the right direction." Abby patted her arm gently. "Do you have family that could help you?"

"I can't tell my family." Her eyes widened. "My father will be so angry he'll kick me out. He won't love me anymore if he knows what I've done."

Abby was appalled; she couldn't imagine a father who would kick out his child when she was in trouble. Her father would never abandon her, no matter what the circumstances.

"Sandy, I know someone who loves you unconditionally. His name is Jesus, and He loves you so much that He died on an old rugged cross to save you. He is the Son of God." Abby squeezed Sandy's hand, a smile on her face.

"You're a Christian?" She shifted on the bench until she faced Abby. "So is my grandmother. She asked me to go to church with her."

"Are you close to your grandmother?"

"Yes. I love Nana, and I know she loves me, but my father wouldn't let me see her after my mother died four years ago. He doesn't believe in God." She fidgeted on the bench. "I hadn't seen Nana until I turned eighteen last month."

"That must have been hard on both of you."

"Yes, it was. I try to spend as much time as I can with her now. She told me that Jesus loves me, too. But I've done things I shouldn't have, and now I'm pregnant and I'm not married. Jesus probably won't love me now." She hung her head.

"Jesus still loves you, and He is willing to forgive you no matter what you've done. That's what I meant when I said His love is unconditional."

Her eyes brightened as she looked up at Abby. "Do you think He might forgive me then?"

"I know He will." Abby smiled. "He loves us so much He is willing to forgive us no matter what we've done."

"I'll have to really think about what you've said." Sandy picked up her purse from the bench beside her. "Maybe I'll go talk with my grandmother and tell her about the baby."

"She loves you, Sandy. I'm sure she'll help you." Abby reached for a small tablet she always kept in her purse. "Here are a few scriptures I'd like you to read." Abby wrote down First John 1:9; Romans 3:23; Romans 10:9; John 3:16; and Romans 10:10, then added her cell phone number and handed the paper to Sandy. "I'll be happy to talk to you some more, or if you feel more comfortable, talk to your grandmother. But you need Jesus in your life. He will help you through this."

"Thank you." Sandy stood and slipped on her coat.

"Will you be all right?" Abby asked as she slipped into her own jacket.

"Yes, I feel better now. I think I'll stay at Nana's tonight."

"That's a good idea. I'll be praying for you." Abby smiled. "Be very careful driving home."

"I will. I have four-wheel drive." She slipped the strap of her purse over her shoulder and started toward the door.

Abby followed her out. Before Sandy left, she turned to Abby with a smile.

"I'm so thankful you came into the restroom today. I'll think about what you've said."

She left, and Abby whispered a prayer. "Please, Father, watch over her and her baby. Bring her to the saving knowledge of Your Son, Jesus Christ. I pray her grandmother will welcome her and give her the help she needs. In Jesus' name I pray, amen."

Nick got up from the bench across from the restroom and walked toward her carrying his bags. From the look on his face, she knew he wondered what had taken her so long.

"Why don't you let me carry that bag for you?" he

asked and glanced toward Sandy as she walked away.

Abby watched the young woman disappear into the crowd and smiled. "That's okay. I can get it; you have enough to carry."

"Is that someone you know?"

"No, but she's upset and needed someone to talk to." Abby told him what had happened in the restroom as they walked across the airport.

"Nice guy." He shook his head. "I hope her grandmother will help her; it's not easy raising a child alone."

Abby glanced over at him, realizing that was something he knew in a personal way.

Chapter 3

Nick glanced up at the sky as they stood waiting for the shuttle. If the weather didn't let up, they were in for a miserable trip. He had to be crazy to let himself get caught in this situation, but he couldn't let Abby drive alone. He knew how stubborn she could be. She would go whether he went along or not. Besides, he owed her something for the way he had treated her fourteen months ago.

He breathed in the fragrance of her perfume, thinking how good it felt to have her sitting next to him again. She hadn't changed much in fourteen months. Five-four and slender built—her reddish-gold hair still hung in curls nearly to her waist. He remembered how her bright blue eyes sparkled when she laughed.

He hoped someday she would let him explain why he broke their engagement to marry Janine and understand that, under the circumstances, he felt it had been his only option.

The driver pulled up next to the SUV and called Nick's name.

"Be careful; it's really slick," Nick said as they stepped out of the van. Ice and snow covered the parking lot, and damp air hit them in the face, chilling them to the bone. Fortunately, he had ignored Abby's protest when they left the airport and held on to her arm, even though she insisted she could make it to the van on her own. She had slipped twice and would have fallen without his support.

"I'll walk you to the car before I get the bags." Nick smiled to himself when she didn't object. By the time Abby was seated, the driver had their luggage unloaded and Nick stowed them in the back of the SUV. She had just fastened her seat belt when he climbed in and started the engine.

Abby wanted to protest and insist that she'd drive. After thinking about it, however, she decided being independent had its merits, but she knew her limitations and Nick had a lot more experience driving in this kind of weather.

"It'll only take a few minutes for the engine to warm up, and I'll turn on the heater," Nick said, rubbing his hands together to try to get warm.

"That would be good. I'm freezing." Abby's teeth were chattering.

Nick slipped off his coat and laid it over her legs. "That should help."

The jacket, still warm from his body heat, felt good.

"But you'll be cold without it." She started to hand it back to him, but he laid his hand over hers. She jerked away as sparks of awareness shot up her arm at his touch. If he noticed her reaction, he didn't respond to it.

"I'll be fine; this sweater is heavy." He turned on the defroster and cranked it up to the highest setting for her. "I'll change it to heat and defrost as soon as it gets warm," he said and pulled out of the parking lot.

Abby smoothed the coat over her knees. He was just as warm and devastating as she remembered, but what they'd had together must remain in the past. She'd made a new life for herself. A happy life. She had been happy, hadn't she? Of course she had.

They had been on the road for about two hours, and Abby realized she'd been dozing when Nick yelled, "Hang on!" jolting her awake as the car jerked to the right, the tires sliding over the ice-coated road. Nick fought the steering wheel, trying to avoid a head-on collision as another car spun into their lane. Abby screamed as the Blazer bumped over the side of the embankment and slammed into the ditch. She jerked forward as her air bag went off. Her seat belt tightened, cutting into her waist and across her shoulder. Dazed and disoriented, for a moment her mind didn't register that Nick was calling her name.

"Abby—Abby! Are you all right?" She felt his hand against her face as he brushed her hair back.

"My cheek hurts." She touched her face and noticed a smear of blood on her hand.

Nick examined her cheek and reached into the back for his medical bag. He deftly opened a package of gauze, folded it into a square, placed it against the open wound, and taped it just below her temple.

"You have a cut here, but I don't think it's deep enough to need sutures. That will hold it until we get someplace where we can do a better job." She squinted as he shone a pin light across the side of her face. The bright light against the darkness hurt her eyes.

"The air bag scratched your face and neck." Nick continued to check her for injuries. "Do you feel dizzy, nauseous, or hurt anywhere else?"

"I don't think so." She sat up suddenly and looked at him. "Are you all right?"

"I'm fine—just a little scratched up, too, from the air bag. But I'm thankful they went off." He set his medical bag back on the seat behind him. "We missed the other car. It spun out of control on the slick pavement. I need to go see about them. Stay here, and I'll be right back."

Nick returned in a few minutes and slid back into the car. "They must have been okay; they're gone."

"Your quick reaction saved our lives." Abby thanked

the Lord she hadn't been driving.

Shaken and still a little disoriented, she peered through the windshield. "It's really nasty out there."

"Yes, and it's getting worse by the minute." He placed his hand under her chin and gently turned her head toward him, checking the bandage on her cheek. Evidently satisfied with the results, he turned the key in the ignition and started the engine. "We need to find a couple of rooms at a hotel and continue on in the morning. It isn't safe to drive anymore tonight. We were fortunate this time. I'm not going to take any more chances with you in the car."

Abby only hesitated for a minute; she knew Nick had a point. As much as she wanted to be home in time to hang the ornaments on Granny's tree, she wanted them to get there safely. It had been a tradition, for as long as she could remember, for the boys to set up the tree the day after Thanksgiving. They hung the lights and glass bulbs. Then on Christmas Eve morning, the girls had hot chocolate with Granny and hung the wooden ornaments. Abby looked forward to it every year.

"You're right." She drew in a shaky breath and picked up the contents of her purse from the floorboard where they had been dumped when the SUV hit the ditch. "We don't want to have another accident."

"I'll do my best to get you there in time." She held the flashlight for Nick while he rolled the airbag up and taped it against the steering wheel, out of the way. "I know how important it is to you."

"I appreciate that." She moved the flashlight over so he could see to roll and tape her air bag to the dash. "But as much as I want to be there, it's more important that we get there in one piece. Granny would have a fit if she knew we were driving in this weather."

"Yes, she would." He took the flashlight and laid it on the seat between them. She figured he wanted it to be handy in case they needed it again. "We need to get going, but we have a problem. Even if we can get out of this ditch, the snow is accumulating so fast on the windshield the wipers are having a difficult time keeping up. I doubt that we can see far enough ahead to find an off-ramp. But we can't stay out in this for long or we'll freeze."

Nick made several attempts to get out of the ditch, and Abby could sense his concern. Even with four-wheel drive, the tires couldn't seem to get traction.

"Slide over here and guide the car. I'm going to try to push it as you give it gas and hope that will be enough." Nick slipped his coat on and went around to the back of the Blazer.

Abby rolled the window down, but she could barely hear Nick with the noise from the wind and snow blowing into her face. He had to be freezing out there.

"Okay, hit the gas real easy," Nick yelled.

She pressed carefully on the gas pedal, and the car eased forward. It hit the pavement slipping and sliding on the ice, heading back toward the ditch. She couldn't see Nick. Panicked, she prayed he'd had time to move out of the way. Her nerves tightened and her palms began to sweat as she fought frantically to keep the car on the road. It bumped the edge of the ditch and spun in a circle before she could get it under control. Abby sat, shaking, with her head resting on the steering wheel, her heart in her throat.

Nick opened the door and laid his hand on her shoulder. "Are you all right?"

Her heart thundered in her chest as she breathed a sigh of relief and thanked the Lord that Nick was okay. "Other than being scared half out of my wits, I'm fine."

She glanced up at him. "You're soaked." She slid over so he could get in.

"Just my coat. I'm dry underneath." He slipped his jacket off once he was in the car and tossed it into the backseat.

Abby fastened her seat belt, and Nick pulled back onto the road. "We'd better start praying," he said. "We aren't going to be able to see to drive for very long in this."

"You drive and I'll pray." Abby bowed her head. "Lord, You know our situation here. Please send us some help. We need to find an exit and a hotel so we can get out of this weather. In Jesus' name we ask, amen."

"Amen," Nick repeated.

A half hour later conditions had not improved. "Nick, this is really scary. I know you can't see any better than I can. A lot of good it does to have a cell phone if it won't work when you need to call for help."

"I know. We must be in a dead zone." Nick cast a sideways glance at Abby and offered a reassuring smile. "There is no other option but to keep driving. Maybe a highway patrol car will come by before too long, to help us."

Fighting the urge to panic, Abby instead returned

the smile. "I hope so, because if we run out of gas, we won't be able to keep the heater going, and without heat we'll freeze before morning."

"It'll be okay." He gave her arm a squeeze. "The Lord will take care of us."

Two hours had gone by. Abby glanced again at the fuel gauge. Every time she looked, it had dropped a little lower. If they didn't find help soon, they would run out of gas.

"There's a truck coming up behind us," Nick said. "When he passes us, I'm going to try to stay behind him. That way I can follow his lights. He sits up high enough he can see better than we can."

Nick stayed behind the trucker for the next several miles. The snow accumulated so thick on the windshield that the trucker's lights were all they could see. The gas gauge, nearing empty, made her more nervous by the minute.

"Look at that!" She could see his bright smile in the reflection from the map light he'd left on. "There must be an exit ahead. He's giving a signal."

"That's great." Her body tensed for a moment. She sure hoped he knew where he was going and wouldn't lead them all into a ditch. They'd just have to trust the Lord in this one. "We can follow him off and find a hotel."

At the bottom of the ramp, a sign indicated Goodland, Kansas, to the left. The truck driver went straight across. "Nick, he is our answer to prayer. Look, he led us off the exit and then went back onto the freeway."

"You're right, Abby." This time Nick's smile was broad, warm, and genuine. "The Lord is faithful. It's amazing how much He loves us and that He always provides our needs."

Nick pulled into a parking space at the Howard Johnson Hotel. Abby scrambled out of the car, determined to pay for the rooms, since Nick had paid for the rental car. As she started toward the lobby, her feet slipped on the icy pavement and she went down hard on her left knee. Before she could get up, Nick stooped down beside her.

"Are you hurt?" He wrapped his arm around her waist.

"I think I'm okay. I just skinned my knee a little." She winced as Nick helped her to her feet.

"Did you bring some snow boots?" She glanced

down as he pointed at her feet. "I don't think those tennis shoes are good on ice."

She glanced over at his feet and realized he had on more suitable shoes with waffle-style soles. No wonder he could get around better than she could.

"I think you've done more than skin your knee a little," Nick said as he looked down at her leg.

Abby realized he was right; blood had soaked through her jeans. Her knee throbbed and burned along with the abrasions on her face and neck from the air bag, but she didn't tell Nick that. He held her arm as he led her to the counter.

"We need two rooms," Nick said, handing the clerk his credit card. "Nonsmoking, please."

The clerk returned Nick's card and gave him the two room keys. The clerk glanced at Abby and back at Nick, noticing their injuries.

"Do you need a doctor?" He started to reach for the phone there on the counter.

"No, I am a doctor," Nick said as he slid his wallet back into his pocket. "But you do need to write up a report, because she fell in your parking lot and injured her knee."

"I'll see to it right away," the clerk said, glancing at the hotel roster, "Dr. Creighton."

Nick helped Abby to the elevator with the bellhop following with their luggage. Abby didn't argue because she didn't want to embarrass Nick in front of the clerk and the bellhop. But she would be taking care of her knee and other injuries herself.

Chapter 4

When Nick and Abby reached their rooms, the bellhop brought their luggage in behind them. He placed her bag next to the closet and took Nick's into the adjoining room. After he pocketed the tip Nick handed him, he left, closing the door.

Nick pulled a folded blanket from the closet shelf and handed it to Abby. "Wrap this around you. You need to slip out of those jeans so I can see what you've done to your knee, and then I'll take care of the places on your cheek and neck. Do you have any others that need attention?"

"Just a few bruises from the seat belt; nothing that won't heal in time. I appreciate the offer, but I can take care of my knee and other injuries myself." The excitement of the day caught up with her suddenly and she slumped, exhausted, into one of the tan chairs across the room from the bed.

"Abby, I can see you're as tired as I am. Let's get this done so we can both get some rest."

"You can go to your room anytime. I'm not stopping you. I can take care of myself," she insisted stubbornly. "I'm sure it's not that bad anyway."

"Let me be the judge of that. I'm the doctor here, and I'm not going anywhere until you let me see your knee." He stood there, clearly determined. "So the longer you resist, the less sleep we'll both get, and tomorrow is going to be another long day."

Abby sighed and closed her eyes for a moment. She knew he meant what he said—if she didn't let him doctor her knee and other injuries, she'd never get to bed. She was just too tired to continue this argument.

"Fine!" She grabbed the blanket and stomped into the bathroom, shutting the door with a loud click. When she pulled her jeans off and got a look at her knee, she sat down on the toilet lid as her stomach lurched. Her head swam, and she wasn't sure if she was going to be sick or faint. She felt like she might do both, so she sat there for a few minutes. When she came out a little later, she had the blanket wrapped securely around her and sat down in the chair. Her stomach felt even queasier, and she was still light-headed. She had wrapped a hand towel around her leg. Her knee was a lot worse than she realized, and she had a huge bruise across her shoulder and her stomach from the seat belt. That bit of information she'd keep to herself—as she'd told Nick earlier, the bruises would heal in time. He didn't need to know exactly what bruises.

When Nick reached over to remove the towel, Abby said, "You'd better lay that under my foot. Otherwise we'll get blood on the carpet."

Nick frowned when he looked at her knee. "You've really done some damage. Are you all right? You look a little pale."

"I'm fine."

Nick studied her for a moment. She didn't look fine.

He'd bet she was nauseated and hoped she wouldn't faint on him. She'd never been very good with cuts of any kind and especially her own. "Sit still then while I get my bag. I'll be right back." He went into his room.

A minute later, he came back with his medical bag and knelt down in front of her, opened an antiseptic pad, and gently washed the area around the deep laceration.

"No matter what I do, it's going to hurt. I think the least intrusive would be to set you on the edge of the tub and wash it in warm water."

"Okay."

She started to stand, but he lifted her before she could protest and carried her into the bathroom and set her on the edge of the tub. When he had her settled, he turned the water on and let it run until he had it adjusted to a comfortable temperature.

"I could have walked in here, you know." Abby looked up at him.

"I know, but this way we didn't drip on the carpet." It was also an excuse to hold her. He loved having her in his arms, even for a short time. "This is going to hurt. I'll do it as gently as I can. Are you ready?"

She took a deep breath and let it out slowly, then

nodded. Nick gritted his teeth when she cried out as the water hit the open wound.

"I'm sorry, honey. I wish there were another way, but it has to be done to keep it from getting infected." Tears rolled down her cheeks, but she didn't complain as he washed the wound with soap and water. He patted it dry, then covered it with an antibiotic ointment and bandaged it. Next, he took care of her cheek and the abrasions on her neck and hands.

"All done. Are you all right?" Nick asked, gently watching her while he waited for an answer.

"Yes. I appreciate you doing this for me." She smiled and dried her feet so she could step out of the tub.

Someone knocked on the door. "That will be room service. I ordered us sandwiches." Nick opened the door and stepped back so the young man could set the tray on the table. Nick gave him a tip, and he left.

"I wasn't sure I'd be able to eat anything, but my stomach feels a little better now, and I'm starving." Abby sat down across from him. They joined hands, and he blessed the food.

"We should try to get an early start. I'd like to leave around seven in the morning if that's all right with you." He tore the paper from a straw and stuck the straw in his drink.

"That's fine. I'll be ready. I just hope the weather is better tomorrow." Abby sipped her root beer.

"I hope it is, too. But at least if it isn't, I'd much rather drive in the daylight." Nick finished his sandwich and leaned back in the chair.

"Even if we don't make it in time to hang the ornaments, I want you to know how much I appreciate you driving through with me, to try to get me there." Abby brushed the hair away from her face.

"I wanted to come with you, and I'm going to do the best I can to get you to Granny's on time. I know how important it is to you to be there." Nick looked at her and smiled.

They had finished eating, so she helped him pick up the papers from the food and tossed them into the wastebasket.

Nick went to his room and took a shower while he waited for Abby to get settled into bed. When he was through, he knocked on the adjoining door.

"Come in." She pulled the blankets up over her.

"Here's some ibuprofen; it'll help with the pain so

you can rest." He handed her a glass of water and two tablets.

"Thank you." Abby took the water and swallowed the tablets.

"Sure; if you need anything, just knock on the door. I'll see you in the morning."

"Okay, good night." She slid down in the bed and closed her eyes just as he went into his room. He glanced back as he shut the door. She looked so beautiful—her image would stay with him the rest of the night.

The next morning Abby had a hard time finding a pair of pants loose enough not to rub against her sore knee. After going through everything in her suitcase, she finally settled on a pair of black sweatpants. They would be comfortable since they would be riding in the car all day.

Nick knocked on the door adjoining their rooms.

"Come in. I'm almost ready," she said as he opened the door.

"How's the knee?" He sank his large frame into a chair across from her and placed the two cups he had in his hand on the small table beside him.

"Sore. I decided to wear my sweatpants. They won't rub it like my jeans would." She glanced over at him as she placed the last of her clothes in her suitcase and zipped it closed.

"I can imagine it is sore. Sweats are a good choice in this case." He smiled sympathetically. "I'll change the bandage when we stop for the night."

"I thought we'd make it home by tonight." She stopped what she was doing and looked at him.

"I don't think so. From the looks of the weather report, we'll have to take it slow. It's snowing too heavy out there for the plows to keep the roads cleared, and we'll be driving in this all the way. I don't want to take any chances, and as long as we make it in by tomorrow evening, you'll be there in time to hang the ornaments," Nick assured her. "Do you want to eat breakfast here or grab something at a fast-food place on the way?"

"Are you hungry?" Abby asked. "If so, we can eat here."

"I have a cup of coffee, so I'm fine either way. I brought you a cup of hot chocolate." He handed her one of the cups he'd set on the table. "Be careful; it's really hot."

"Thanks. With this I'll be fine for a while, so we can wait and stop on the way." She reached for the chocolate and slid the lid open, blowing into the top to cool it before taking a sip.

As they got into the Blazer, Abby noticed the dark clouds hovering overhead. The countryside was covered in thick layers of snow. It was still coming down steadily, and it didn't look like it would let up any time soon. Normally she loved the snow and enjoyed the beauty of it, but not when they had to be out driving in it.

She glanced at Nick as he pulled out of the icy parking lot. His strong hands on the steering wheel expertly maneuvered the SUV on the slick road. She thanked the Lord that he had come with her—even though being this close to him rekindled feelings she had hoped were long gone. She knew there was a reason for their being on the same plane. She didn't believe in coincidence; the Lord had a reason for everything that happened.

Abby adjusted the sweatshirt she had draped over her legs and moved her purse from her lap to the floorboard.

"Are you warm enough?" Nick started to reach to turn the heater up.

"Yes, I'm fine. The heat feels good."

Abby realized at that moment the reason she'd avoided dating the last fourteen months. She had declined every dinner invitation she'd received. She didn't have any interest in going out with anyone who had asked her. Now she knew why. She still had feelings for Nick. Sitting so close to him, she could smell the fresh scent of his cologne, a familiar fragrance, her favorite. Memories flooded into her thoughts of the happy times they'd spent together. She shook her head—time to get her mind back where it belonged. She couldn't afford to think about the past. It hurt too much.

"What do you do for a living in the little town fifty miles inland from San Francisco?" Nick asked. "Tell me about your job and where you live."

This subject she felt safe discussing. "I have a small one-bedroom apartment in a town called Tracy. I manage a travel agency in the mall there. My office is about two miles from my home, so I don't have very far to drive each day to get to work. I can park just outside the door, so I don't have to be out in the wind and weather when it's nasty out."

"Manager, huh? Well, that doesn't surprise me,

since you had your own agency back home. Do you like your job and living in Tracy?"

She knew what he wanted to know—if she was happy.

"Yes, I do." She took a sip of her hot chocolate. "The owner of the agency only comes in occasionally. She is good to me, and the agents I work with are nice people."

"Have you ever regretted giving up your agency and moving away from Pierce City?" Nick sipped his coffee.

"To be honest, I'd have to say yes. But I'm adjusting."

"I'm sorry, Abby, for everything." His voice grew soft.

"Nick, that was a long time ago." She squirmed in the seat. "A subject better left alone."

Lord, I believe Abby is the mate You've chosen for me, and You know how much I love her. Help me to be patient, to be able to win her trust and love once again. Please give me an opportunity to make things right between us, Nick prayed silently.

Just as he ended his prayer, he heard a loud *pop*, and

the SUV began to swerve all over the road. He knew immediately they had blown a tire. He took his foot off the gas but didn't hit the brakes, allowing the vehicle to slow down as he guided it to the side of the road.

Abby's blue eyes widened. "What happened?"

"We've blown a tire," Nick said and unfastened his seat belt. "I hope and pray there's a spare in the back."

He climbed out of the car, and his boots sunk to his ankles in the deep snow. He shivered in spite of his heavy jacket. Wind and snow pelted him in the face as he made his way to the back of the Blazer. He opened the hatch to look for a spare and jack to change the tire—not his favorite thing to do in this weather. It didn't look like he had to worry about it; they didn't have a jack. He closed the hatch and climbed back inside. The warmth from the heater felt wonderful as he rubbed his hands together in an attempt to get the feeling back into his frozen fingers.

"We have a bit of a problem." Nick sighed and laid his arm across the steering wheel. "There's a spare, but we don't have a jack."

"Great!" Abby turned toward him in the seat. "Now what are we going to do?"

"I'll try my cell phone and call AAA. Maybe we're in a place where it will work this time." Nick pulled his phone out of his pocket, flipped it open, dialed, and waited while it rang.

Please, Lord, I pray it will go through. We need some help here.

"It's ringing."

"Hello, AAA road service, how can I help you?" a woman's soft voice asked.

"We're on Highway 70 just a few miles from Russell, Kansas. We've blown a tire."

"Do you have a spare, sir?" she asked.

"Yes, but we don't have a jack and we need some fuel. We're almost out of gas. We're in a light blue Chevy Blazer." He then gave her the license number shown on the rental agreement and estimated the closest highway mile post. Nick wasn't leaving it to chance that another SUV would be mistaken for theirs.

"I'll send a rig out as soon as I can, but it may be a little while. We're swamped with calls. We have been all morning. There are a lot of people stuck in this weather."

"Okay. Thank you. I'm afraid we won't be going

anywhere, so we'll be right here when he's free," Nick said and closed his phone before slipping it back into his pocket.

"Well, that didn't sound too promising." Nick frowned. "I have a feeling we may be here awhile. They're very busy. She said she'd send a rig as soon as one becomes available."

Nick locked the doors and turned on the flashers. "I guess we might as well get as comfortable as we can." He slumped down and laid his head against the headrest of his seat.

"Abby, I'd like to explain to you why I broke our engagement." He closed his eyes and waited, hoping she'd agree to listen.

"Nick." She hesitated as if she were thinking about it, and his hopes rose, but in the next moment, she dashed them completely. "Please, let's not talk about that—not right now."

He sighed, gritting his teeth to hold back his disappointment. "All right, but one of these days we need to talk about it."

"Well, that may be, but please, not now."

He heard the crack in her voice. This was hard for her.

He was to blame for that hurt, and his chest tightened with regret. Still he was frustrated at her continued refusal to listen to him. He hoped his explanation would make it a little easier for her. Maybe it would help to know that he had a good reason, as unfair as it was, for what he'd done. That is, if she'd ever allow him to give her his explanation.

Nick closed his eyes, and the memories of that night flooded his mind. Janine had come to him after his brother had been killed in Kuwait. She made him promise he would never reveal what she planned to tell him. After he gave his word, she told him about her pregnancy and that the child she carried belonged to his brother. She wanted to draw up a business arrangement with him. If he would marry her and give the baby his name, she would sign papers giving him sole custody, along with an annulment the day after the child's birth. If he wouldn't agree, she would have an abortion. He cringed even now at the thought of her destroying the baby.

Abby had shown such compassion to the young girl at the airport, and he loved her even more for it. He prayed that she would allow him to explain and would show him some of that compassion—and understand that he'd had no choice in the decision he'd made the night he'd broken their engagement.

Chapter 5

"It's been two hours since we called." Abby shivered and wrapped her coat more securely around her. "I wonder how much longer it'll be before they get here."

"I don't know, but surely it won't be too much longer. I'll start the engine and turn the heater back on for a little while so you can get warm."

"I'm okay. I know we're low on gas and you're trying to conserve what we have. If we run out, we won't have any heat. I can wait a little longer."

"It won't take that much to run it for a few minutes. You're freezing, and I don't want you to get sick."

"Nick, I'm really sorry I got you into this. It was a foolish idea to try to drive in this weather. Now you're out here in the middle of nowhere, stuck, freezing in the snow, and it's all my fault. I didn't want to disappoint Granny, but she wouldn't want us to risk our lives to get there."

"I came because I wanted to, Abby. I knew the risks. Besides, we're going to be fine. AAA will be here before long, and we'll soon be on our way again."

Abby sighed and leaned back against the seat. Nick had always been such a special person, and she could see that hadn't changed. She didn't know if she'd ever be able to trust him again, but during the time they'd been together on this trip, she had regained her respect for him. After all, he didn't have to come with her, yet he hadn't hesitated, even with the severe weather conditions. He'd also done everything he could to help and protect her. She kept thinking about the situation they found themselves in. What if help didn't get here in time and this would be the last chance she had to find out what had caused Nick to break their engagement fourteen months ago and marry Janine? Maybe she should listen to his explanation. Otherwise she might not ever know.

She watched him for a moment. He looked so handsome, relaxed there next to her, his head resting on the seat. Just looking at him took her breath away. She still had feelings for him, but he had hurt her, and she was leery of him. Although, if she were honest with herself, she had to admit she was glad he had come with her. Even though she wasn't ready to accept him back into her life, she didn't want him completely out of it, either. Maybe what he was going to tell her would make a difference. She'd listen to him and then reevaluate the situation.

"Nick," Abby said softly, "I've thought about what you said earlier, and I've decided, if you want to explain what happened fourteen months ago, I'm ready to listen."

He opened his eyes and scooted up in his seat as he turned toward her. She swallowed nervously. Had she made a mistake? Would what he had to say make things worse? Whether it did or not, she had to know.

Abby sat quietly and listened as Nick explained exactly what had happened with Janine.

He flipped the map light on so he could see her face.

The anguish he saw there and knowing he had caused it nearly ripped his heart out. Closing his eyes, he paused for a minute longer to regain his composure. He looked at her and said, "I couldn't let her destroy my brother's baby, Abby. Scotty is all I have left of Nathan. I didn't have any other choice. I just couldn't let her have an abortion. I'm sorry. If there had been any other way, believe me, I would have taken it. I never meant to hurt you."

Nick paused for a moment to give Abby time to take in all he'd just shared with her, praying she would understand and forgive him. He loved her so much. She was his life. He hoped they could still have a future together. When she didn't say anything, he continued.

"Abby, I felt terrible, and my heart ached and still does about the way I treated you. I had no choice but to break our engagement without giving you an explanation." At the sight of the tears welling in her eyes, he ran his hand through his hair and swallowed hard before continuing.

"I still have a difficult time understanding how my brother could have gotten himself into a situation like this. Nathan's Christian principles were as strong as mine are. But he loved Janine to distraction, and I have no doubt this child belongs to him." He paused and swallowed again, having a hard time keeping his own emotions under control while he finished what he had to say.

"I had no choice. I signed the necessary papers, agreeing to keep her secret until after the annulment and she'd left the area."

Abby glanced up at him as tears spilled over and ran down her face. She impatiently wiped them away. Talking about this was hard for her. Nick knew her well enough to know that she would feel compassion for him even though she didn't want to. He'd hurt her that night, and she wasn't sure she could trust him. He couldn't blame her for not ever wanting to suffer like that again.

Nick saw tears well in her eyes again and felt like a heel, hoping as he finished his story she would understand and it would ease some of the pain and disappointment he knew she was feeling.

"There's something else that Janine failed to tell me—one very important factor," Nick continued as Abby reached into her purse for a tissue. "Janine had a severe heart condition, and the doctor advised against her carrying the child, explaining that if she carried the baby to term, she'd never live through the strain of childbirth." He had to stop and clear his throat. His emotions were about to get the better of him in spite of his efforts to keep them under control.

"She left a letter with her lawyer to be given to me after her death. In the letter, Janine explained that she loved Nathan, and she wanted their baby to have a chance."

"If she loved him and the baby so much. . ." Abby paused for a moment and looked at him. "How could she even consider having an abortion?"

"I asked myself that same question. Looking back, I'm sure she wouldn't have had the abortion if I'd refused, but I didn't know her well enough to realize that. She probably felt that threatening to do so was the only way to guarantee that I would agree to her terms. She knew I would love and give her baby the home she wanted for him. In her letter she asked for my forgiveness for placing me in such a position. She just didn't know what else to do; she had to know her baby would be loved and cared for after her death." Nick shifted to a more comfortable position.

"In the letter she also gave me permission to tell you the whole story." He didn't add that Janine's letter said she hoped he and Abby would reconcile and raise the baby together. Nick would keep that part a secret for now and pray for Abby's love and understanding—along with the right time to share that information with her.

"It was just a business arrangement, Abby. We were never intimate. It wasn't a real marriage. I had an obligation to my brother's child, and I couldn't see any other way. I'd made a promise not to reveal Janine's secret before I realized what it would cost us. I never dreamed that what she was about to tell me would change our plans."

She was quiet for so long that Nick had decided she wasn't going to comment at all, but then she turned in the seat and faced him.

"I understand that you were faced with a difficult choice, Nick, but you devastated my world. I loved you so much—you were my whole life. I respect your having the courage to honor a promise, but we were engaged. You had an obligation to honor me, too, and I feel you owed me an honest explanation that night.

What you did to me was unfair, and I'm sorry, but I don't trust you not to hurt me again."

"I'm sorry, too, Abby. Not telling you the truth was a terrible mistake. I know that now, and I hope you know I would never hurt you intentionally. I love you. I've never stopped loving you. Can you honestly tell me that you no longer have any feelings for me? If you can truthfully tell me that, then I'll take you home and I won't bother you anymore."

Abby squirmed in the seat next to him. He prayed it was because she couldn't bring herself to sever their relationship completely and she'd admit that to him.

After a moment or two, she sighed. "I can't tell you that. I do still have feelings. But I'm not willing to pursue them right now. I need time to think and time to pray. I can't promise anything."

"I understand how you feel, and I'll give you all the time you need." As hard as it would be to wait, at least that gave him some hope.

Nick glanced up as lights reflected in the rearview mirror. "I think that's our tow truck. Stay inside here where it's warm." He grabbed his jacket from the back-seat, opened the door, and stepped out as the large truck pulled up and parked in front of their SUV.

"I'm sure glad to see you." Nick walked up to him.

"Yeah, it's a bit too chilly out here to sit for very long. You have a spare?" the driver asked.

"Yes, but it's a rental, and we don't seem to have a jack." Nick opened the trunk and pulled out the spare tire. The tow truck driver took the tire, rolled it over to the flat, and proceeded to change it. Nick sure was glad this wasn't his line of work, and he felt for the young man having to be out in weather like this changing tires. But he was certainly thankful for his help. When the driver finished changing the tire, he added gas to the fuel tank. Nick gave him his AAA card, signed the necessary papers, and climbed back into the SUV with Abby.

"Man, it's cold out there. Even with my gloves on, my hands are frozen." He blew on his fingers to try to warm them and then started the engine. "We can use the heater again. He gave us enough gas to get us to the next town, which he said would take about a half hour from here."

With the snow coming down so hard, it was difficult to see very far ahead. Nick carefully maneuvered the Blazer onto the icy road. They certainly didn't want to wind up in another ditch.

This was crazy. Anyone with any sense wouldn't be out driving in this weather at all. But he'd do just about anything to make Abby happy, and he knew how important it was to her to be at Granny's for the hanging of the ornaments and the family Christmas gathering. He'd pray for safety and do his very best to get her there on time and in one piece.

"That heat feels good." Nick kept one hand on the steering wheel and held the other in front of the vent to warm his fingers.

"Yes, it does. I'm freezing, and I haven't been out of the car. I can't even imagine how cold you are."

"I'm beginning to thaw out now. As long as I've known you, you've prayed for a white Christmas. I presume that hasn't changed." Nick grinned. "You sure got your wish this year."

Abby laughed. "No, it hasn't changed. I always pray for snow at Christmas. But I'm afraid I got more than I bargained for this time." As her laughter faded, she said, "I just hope it doesn't keep any of the family from making it this year."

"I wondered, now that all four of you girls have moved away, if you would all make it to Granny's this year." Nick turned the steering wheel slightly when they began to slide a little on the slick, icy road. He felt Abby stiffen next to him and then relax as the car stopped skidding before she answered him.

"It's been touch and go for a while, but at least two of us will be there. Amanda is living in Oklahoma City; she's the closest to home. She's a real estate agent there. She's bringing a friend named Josh Randall. Lauren called Granny and said she couldn't come, but I keep hoping she'll change her mind at the last minute and make it after all. You remember Jeff Warren?"

"Sure, we went to school together." Nick corrected the car again and slowed down just a little. The roads were getting worse. He didn't know how much longer they would be able to continue to drive in this.

"He and Lauren have been best friends for years. When Granny called and told him Lauren wasn't coming home for Christmas, he decided to go to St. Louis where she's living now and see if he could change her mind. I'm praying he'll be successful."

"I'm sure Granny was pleased about that. Where

does Lauren work in St. Louis?"

"She's a librarian there, and she loves it. Granny is thrilled that two of us are coming for sure. She's upset over Lauren and Casey, but she's praying and is hopeful they'll make it, even if it's at the last minute. Casey called and said she couldn't come. She's living in Cade's Point, California, which is a town by the beach not too far from Los Angeles. She works for a large clothing company. Part of her job is creating the front window design for the holidays, and she feels she needs to be there for the Christmas party. I keep praying something will change. If the reason she isn't coming has to do with someone special she wants to spend Christmas with, then I hope she'll decide to come and bring him with her." She grinned, her eyes lighting with excitement. "It would be great if the four of us could be there after all."

"Yes, and if that happens, we'll have a full house this year." Nick smiled. "I hope it works out. Everyone loves Granny, and it's hard to think of disappointing her."

"I know, I just can't imagine being anywhere else for Christmas. I've always been home with my family. I guess we're really fortunate." Abby opened a package of gum, offered him a piece, and took one for herself before placing it back into her purse. "So many people don't have a family to be with."

Chapter 6

Nick thought about the Christmases he had spent with his family. Now his brother was gone, and they would never have another Christmas with him. Yes, Abby was fortunate to have her family all together to celebrate with. He had to try to concentrate now on making new traditions with Scotty. He would be the best father he could possibly be and try to make Scotty's world as happy a place as he could for the little guy.

Nathan, I'll do the best I can to make your son a good home. I'll raise him to know the Lord, the way I know you would have if you had been given the chance.

Abby glanced over at Nick. She hadn't thought about how he must feel. This would be a difficult Christmas for him and his family without his brother, and she knew how much Nick had loved him. They had been very close growing up, only eighteen months apart. He'd miss Nathan terribly.

She remembered how hard it had been for Nick when Nathan told him he had enlisted and that he'd be deployed overseas. Nick had taken every extra shift available at the hospital to keep himself busy. She'd hardly seen him for weeks after Nathan left. Nick came to see her one evening and apologized for neglecting her. He explained that he and Nathan had talked just before his brother shipped out. Nick told her that after spending a lot of time in prayer, he'd finally come to terms with his brother's decision. Even though it would be hard, he'd felt he could accept it. Then Nathan had been killed shortly after his deployment.

"Nick, I'm so sorry. I didn't think. I know it's hard for you this year. I'm glad you're both going to be with us for Christmas instead of being alone. By the way, where are your mother and dad?"

"Mom and Dad are taking a cruise. They just couldn't handle being at home this year for the holidays. They needed something different. Since we lost Nathan in October, we didn't celebrate the holidays last year. And this will be the first Christmas since Janine's death, so it's been hard for them—for all of us—but having Scotty helps."

"I can certainly understand their feelings." She couldn't imagine losing either of her brothers.

"Abby." Nick interrupted her thoughts. "My parents don't know that Scotty isn't mine. No one does but you."

"Why?" Abby asked, confused that Nick would keep this from his parents.

"I can see by the shocked look on your face you don't understand," Nick said.

"No, I don't understand." Abby looked over at him. "I would think it would be a joy to them to know they had a part of Nathan in his son."

"Janine didn't want anyone to think ill of Nathan, and she was afraid they would if they knew the truth about Scotty. You know how some people are in a small town. We love them all, but you always have a few that gossip every chance they get. Martha Ogalberry would have a field day with this. I can just see it. She'd tell Henrietta Stallings, and it would be all over the church in no time."

"Yes, you're right. I can understand her not wanting you to tell anyone else. But I know your parents would be thrilled to know they still have a part of your brother in his son."

"I'm sure they would, Abby, but I promised Janine I wouldn't tell anyone. The letter she left gave me permission to tell only you."

"Nick, I understand your loyalty to Janine. But I think under these circumstances, you need to think about what your brother would have wanted. You have to make a decision as to what is best here. She was trying to protect your brother's reputation, and I can relate to that, but maybe she didn't stop to think about how much it would mean to your mother and dad. They would really benefit from knowing you have Nathan's son. You don't have to tell anyone else, so that way you can still keep her secret." Abby thought about what she had said and wished she'd kept her mouth shut. She was no longer a part of Nick's life; she probably shouldn't have commented at all.

"Nick, I'm sorry. This isn't any of my business. Please just forget what I said and do what you think is best."

"If I hadn't wanted you involved, I wouldn't have told you any of this. I value your opinion, and you may be right, but I have to think about it and pray before I make a decision."

"I think it's a good idea to let the Lord guide you in this. That way you know you won't make the wrong choice."

A little while later, Abby was getting hungry. With the time lost on the flat tire, they had missed breakfast, and it was now well past time for lunch. Her stomach growled audibly. Heat filled her cheeks in embarrassment, and she hoped Nick hadn't heard. But he chuckled.

"Obviously you're hungry. I think we need to find someplace to get you something to eat. It shouldn't be much farther to the exit. When we get into town, we can get some gas and find a restaurant. I'm getting hungry, too."

They took the next off-ramp and pulled into a

service station so Nick could fill the gas tank. Next door to the station, they found a small country restaurant. He parked the Blazer and shut off the engine. The cold wind whipped Abby's hair into her face as she stepped out of the car, causing her to shiver. She sniffed appreciatively upon entering the cheery dining area with its shiny white walls, red checked curtains, and tablecloths to match. Something smelled wonderful, and her stomach growled again.

Nick grinned as she felt the heat creep into her cheeks. "I'm sorry," she apologized.

"You're hungry; you can't help that." Nick pulled a chair out for her to sit down and then sank into the one across from her. On every table sat a candle, a vase with two poinsettias—one white, one red—with a sprig of Christmas greens in each. A red-and-green-checked bow decorated the vase.

Across the room sat a large stuffed Santa and Mrs. Claus in a rocking chair.

"Look at that, Nick. Aren't they cute?"

"Yes they are. You obviously haven't lost your love for Santa." He chuckled.

Abby grinned. "No, I guess in that respect I'll always

be a little girl at heart. I love Christmas."

Abby glanced around. In front of a large picture window stood a Christmas tree tall enough to reach the ceiling, decorated with red and green lights, bulbs, and lots of small wooden ornaments. It gave the room a festive glow.

The waitress came to the table, set two glasses of water in front of them, and handed them each a menu. "Hi, welcome to Annie's Kitchen." She smiled brightly. "My name is Ellie. What can I get for you to drink today?"

"Root beer for me, please." Abby smiled and placed her purse on the chair next to her.

"I'll have a Dr Pepper." Nick slipped off his jacket and hung it on the back of his chair.

"I'll be back to take your orders in a few minutes." The waitress left to get their drinks while they looked at the menu.

Abby opened her napkin and spread it across her lap before she sat back to read her copy of the menu. "I think I'll have a cheeseburger and fries."

"Sounds good. I'll have the same." Nick took her menu and set them on the edge of the table. When the waitress returned a few minutes later with their soft drinks, Nick gave her their orders. She took both menus and headed toward the kitchen.

"I told you all about my job and apartment in California." Abby reached for her glass of water and took a drink, more for something to do than because she was thirsty. "So now it's your turn. Are you still working at the hospital?" Nick's cologne wafted toward her. The familiar scent brought back memories of meals they had shared in the past, causing her heart to ache with what should have been as she waited for him to answer.

"No, I decided about six months ago to take my dad up on his offer and go into practice with him and your brother. There are four of us sharing the medical building now. Brad Collins joined our office. He specializes in obstetrics and gynecology. He moved here from Kansas City shortly after you left. He's a good doctor, one of the best in his field, and we were thankful to have him join us."

"That's great. And your joining your dad should have made him happy. I know that's been his desire ever since you started med school. It's convenient for the patients, too, to have a general practitioner, a pediatrician, an orthopedist, and an OB/GYN all in one office."

"Yes, it's working out well, and I'm happy as I can be. But my life will never be completely happy without you." Nick looked directly at her, making her uncomfortable. She squirmed in her chair and quickly changed the subject.

"Do you have an apartment or a house?"

Nick sighed at her response and took a sip of the water to wet his dry throat before he answered. "Janine had a rental, a two-story house. I lived there until just recently. I occupied the upstairs, and she lived downstairs. Five months ago I bought forty acres and had a five-bedroom house built. It's a two-story with a full basement, and I had a barn with ten stalls built back behind the house for the horses." He smiled.

"You have horses?" she cried softly. Riding Granny's horse, Cody, out across her twenty-acre farm was one of the things Abby missed.

"Six of them and two more on the way. It's between Pierce City and Wentworth. You'll have to come out and see it and the horses."

The waitress came back and placed their orders in front of them, along with bottles of ketchup and mustard. "Let me know if there is anything else I can get for you."

"Abby, is there anything else you want?" Nick looked over at her.

"No, thank you. This is fine." She smiled up at the waitress, and the girl nodded her head in response as she walked away.

"I'd love to see your place and the horses while I'm here." Abby smiled at Nick as she unwrapped her straw and put it in her root beer, trying to ignore the information about Janine and that she was ever a part of Nick's life. "Tell me about Scotty. What does he look like, and who keeps him when you're working?"

His gaze softened. "Scotty is the delight of my life. He looks just like Nathan. He hardly ever cries except when he's hungry, and he's been sleeping all night since he was six weeks old. I'm very fortunate. He's a good baby. I have a daytime housekeeper-nanny, Maggie Shepherd; she takes care of Scotty and keeps the house up."

"I know Maggie; she's a nice lady." Abby studied Nick as she ate her cheeseburger and fries. She could see the love in his eyes when he talked about the baby. Nick and Nathan had looked so much alike, people would never question whether Scotty was Nick's.

"Yes, Maggie's a special person. She's warm and loving, and she takes good care of Scotty. I don't have to worry about him when I'm away, like I have been the last few days for the convention and now our travel delay. Maggie loves him as if he were another one of her grandchildren. She's been keeping him since he was born, so he loves her, too. I'm as comfortable leaving him with her for a few days as I am leaving him with my mother."

"Have you thought about what you're going to tell him when he's old enough to understand? Are you going to tell him about your brother, or are you going to raise him as yours?"

"I've thought about it a lot. I'll probably tell him about Nathan, but we'll see when the time comes."

"If you do decide to tell him, have you thought about how your parents are going to feel when they realize you've kept this from them?"

Nick looked at her for a moment before he answered. "I've thought about that, too, but I haven't come to a decision yet." He took the last bite of his cheeseburger and finished his Dr Pepper.

Abby didn't say any more. She just prayed he'd make the right decision. When he saw that she was finished, he reached for the bill. "I'll pay it." Abby grabbed for it, but Nick beat her to it.

"I've got it." Nick pulled out his wallet and headed to the counter.

Not wanting to make a scene, Abby didn't argue with him. She waited until they got into the car.

"Nick, I'm paying that bill," she insisted. "You paid for the food yesterday. It's my turn."

"We can settle up when we get to Granny's, okay?"

Abby hesitated. "All right, but only if you promise you'll let me pay half."

"Fine." Nick started the car and turned on the heater. "It's still snowing and getting deeper by the minute. I don't know how much longer we can drive in this."

"How far are we from Pierce City?" Abby wrapped the sweatshirt back around her legs.

"It's about six and a half hours. I hope the plows have been out on the highway."

Nick switched over to four-wheel drive and pulled

out onto the road. "From the looks of the weather, even if they have, they'll have a hard time keeping up, so I doubt we'll make it that soon."

Abby closed her eyes and laid her head back on the seat to rest for a few minutes. The next thing she knew, she'd been napping for three of the five hours they'd been on the road. She sat up and looked out the window, watching the snowflakes continue to drift over the countryside. The quiet seemed almost eerie. Nick reached over and turned on the radio, searching until he found a station playing soft music.

Abby appreciated the break in the silence until the song came on that had been playing the night Nick had asked her to marry him. The happiest night of her life—so she had thought at the time. He had taken her out to dinner at a nice restaurant in Springfield. When they'd finished their meal, he had flipped open a small, black velvet box, and inside lay the most beautiful engagement ring she had ever seen. A solitaire diamond encircled with emeralds. She hadn't even hesitated when he'd asked her to marry him. She immediately said yes, beaming with excitement because she'd loved him more than anything. Everything had been wonderful in her world. Amazing how things can quickly change.

"Where are we?" she asked, her voice flat.

"Are you okay?" Nick glanced at her.

"Yes, I'm fine." But she wasn't. Tears filled her eyes, and she blinked rapidly to try to keep them from escaping and rolling down her face. She thought she had put this behind her, but obviously not, since just hearing that one song brought all of the hurt hurling back in one swoop.

"This is Vinita, Oklahoma. We're about an hour and a half from home. But in this weather it will probably take us a couple of hours to drive it." Nick leaned forward slightly. The snow had accumulated so thick on the windshield that Abby knew he could hardly see through it. "A sign back there said there's a Holiday Inn Express & Suites at the next exit two miles ahead. I can't see a foot in front of me. I thought maybe we could make it on in tonight since we're close to home, but it isn't safe to drive any farther. We need to book two rooms for tonight and pray the weather will be better in the morning. Then we can drive on in tomorrow. If we get up early, we can still be to Granny's in time for you to hang the ornaments with the girls."

"I hope the other girls are there." Abby worried about them, knowing they were traveling in this weather, too. The snow continued to fall, and there didn't seem to be any hope of it ending any time soon.

"I'll call my parents when we get settled in our rooms to see if they made it yet and let them know where we are. I'll be glad when we get there. It's almost as if we're out here alone with nowhere to go. It's a strange feeling. Are you sure we can make it another two miles in this?" Abby leaned forward and squinted to try to see through the windshield better.

"Nick, stop!" she cried.

Chapter 7

Nick didn't dare slam on the brakes, so he tapped them several times, gradually bringing the SUV to a stop. They passed a car that had slid nose first into the ditch. Since the taillights were still on, the accident must have just happened. He pulled over to the side of the road, out of the way of any traffic that might be coming, and backed up carefully until they were just ahead of the car. "Stay here, Abby." Nick slipped into his jacket. "I'll go see if anyone is injured and if there is anything I can do."

"I should go with you; you might need some help." She started to unfasten her seat belt.

"There's no need for you to get out in this weather unless it's necessary. I'll go check and let you know if I need help, okay?"

"All right, I'll wait here. But please be careful."

Nick nodded and shut the door. Wind and snow hit him square in the face, instantly chilling him to the bone. He slipped and slid all the way down the side of the ditch, sinking almost to his knees in the cold, wet snow making it difficult to move. Finally, he reached the door of the car. Concern filled him when he didn't see any attempt being made to get out of the ditch or any movement at all. He knocked on the window; it seemed several minutes went by before it rolled down just a tiny crack. "Are you all right? I'm a doctor; is anyone hurt?"

"We're okay, but the car is stuck," the man behind the wheel said. "We called AAA. They're sending a truck out, but the dispatcher said it would be about thirty minutes before it could get here. We appreciate your stopping. We have a full tank of fuel, so we can run the heater. We'll be okay."

"I'm glad you're not hurt. Merry Christmas." Nick waved and headed back up the side of the bank to the SUV. He opened the door and climbed in beside Abby.

"Are you all right, and is anyone hurt in the other car?" Abby handed him some tissue to wipe the snow off of his face.

"No, fortunately. They're just stuck. A tow truck is on its way." Nick slipped out of his wet jacket and laid it out in the backseat again to dry. There wasn't much he could do about his wet pants, but they'd be at the hotel soon. He started the engine and eased back onto the road. He'd be glad when they got to Granny's. This was the worst trip he'd ever made, and he wasn't looking forward to battling this storm the rest of the way home. Driving in this weather was just plain foolish. He'd much rather be sitting in front of a fire with Abby than out here on an icy highway. Of course, there was no way for him to know whether she would ever agree to sit by a fire with him again in the future. That thought didn't set well with him at all.

Abby stared out the window at the snow-covered countryside. Snow this time of year made it seem more like Christmas, but she didn't like driving in it. She watched Nick as he expertly maneuvered the SUV on the slick road. She had never met anyone who even held a candle to him, as the saying went. She realized, having spent all of this time in such close quarters with him, that she loved him just as much as she had when he'd broken their engagement. She didn't want to love him, but she'd be lying to herself if she denied her feelings any longer. But was she ready to rekindle their relationship? She didn't know the answer to that question. She'd pray and ask the Lord to guide her and help her to make the right decision.

"There's the exit for the hotel." Nick flipped on the turn signal and took the off-ramp. "I'll be glad to get out of this weather and into dry clothes. I just hope it's better in the morning."

"I hope so, too." Abby unfastened her seat belt as Nick parked in front of the hotel and turned off the engine. He came around and opened her door while she put on her jacket. She took the hand he offered to steady her on the slick pavement. She certainly didn't want another skinned knee.

The clerk signed them in and handed them their keys, and they went up to their appointed rooms. After the bellhop left, Nick knocked on Abby's door.

"Abby, it's me," Nick said.

Abby went to open the door. "Come on in."

"Are you hungry?" Nick asked and reached for the room service menu.

"Yes, I'm starving. I hope they have something good in there."

"Well, let's take a look and see." He sat down beside her on the blue sofa and opened the menu, holding it where they could both read it.

"I think I'll have a turkey sandwich and chips," Abby said and leaned back against the sofa. "That will be fairly light. I don't want to eat something heavy and then go to bed on a really full stomach."

"Yeah, I agree. I think I'll order a club sandwich." He laid the menu on the dresser and reached for the phone. "Do you want milk or a soda?"

"Milk, please. If I drink a soda I'll be up all night." She sighed.

Nick dialed the room service number listed on a small card sitting next to the phone and ordered their supper. "She said it would be about twenty minutes. I think I'll go take a quick shower."

"I'm going to take one, too, and then call my parents

to let them know where we are."

After Nick went to his room, Abby slipped out of her sweatpants. She covered her injured knee with a piece of plastic bag and the tape Nick gave her to keep it dry while she showered. The warm water felt so good. She didn't know when she'd been so tired. She washed her hair, then stepped out onto the small rug. After drying with the large, fluffy towel, she removed the tape and plastic bag from her knee and threw it in the trash. When she was finished, she dressed in a pair of green sweats and went out to call her parents.

Nick knocked on the door just as she hung up the phone. She opened it, and a young man followed Nick in with their orders and placed them on the table. He thanked Nick for the tip and left.

They sat down at the table, and Nick said a blessing. Abby opened the lids, handed Nick his plate, and placed a napkin in her lap.

"I just talked with Maggie, and Scotty is doing great. I sure miss the little guy. Did you get a chance to call your folks?" Nick asked.

"Yes, they were relieved to hear from me and know we're okay." She took a bite of her sandwich, chewed it, and swallowed. "Amanda and her friend Josh arrived safely last night. I'm so thankful to know they're all right. They haven't heard any more from Lauren and Casey."

"I'm sorry. I know you're disappointed. I'm glad Amanda and her friend made it okay, and I'll be glad when we get there, as well. Anything can happen in this kind of weather. It isn't safe to be traveling in it."

They finished their meal, and Nick helped Abby clean up the trash.

"Let's change the bandage on your knee before I go to my room." Nick sat in a chair and opened his medical bag. Abby pulled the leg of her sweats up enough that he could remove the tape and gauze. She closed her eyes and braced herself, expecting the gauze to stick to the wound and pull the top off. When she didn't feel any pain, she opened her eyes, surprised to see the bandages already in the trash. Whatever Nick had used on her knee hadn't stuck to the bandage. Relieved, she leaned back and relaxed while he put on a new one. He smelled so good. Being here with him stirred her senses. His strong hands were gentle as he worked on her knee. The touch of his fingers on her skin sent a tingle of awareness up her spine.

"It looks pretty good—no sign of infection," Nick said, jolting her from her thoughts as he put his supplies back into his bag and closed the top.

She was thankful for the interruption. What was she doing? She couldn't allow herself to think like that.

"I called the desk and requested a wake-up call for five o'clock. That should give us plenty of time to get ready to leave and still make it to Granny's in time for you to hang the ornaments." He cupped her chin in his hand and placed a kiss on her cheek. "Good night. I'll see you in the morning," he said and left, locking her door behind him.

Abby lay awake for a long time, thinking and praying. She knew there was a reason the Lord had brought her and Nick together. Was it in His plan for them to have a future? Could she put what happened with Janine in the past and give Nick another chance? She had been so jealous of Janine, but the thought of her dying so young disturbed Abby. She'd never wanted anything like that to happen. She couldn't help but feel bad. It had to have been hard for Janine to know she was dying and that she would have to leave her baby to be raised by someone else.

Abby's heart ached at the thought of what she must have gone through. Nick would be a good father to Scotty, but a child also needed a mother. She sat up in the bed. Was this the Lord's plan? The reason He had brought them together? Did He want her and Nick to raise Scotty?

The next morning Nick knocked on Abby's door at five thirty. When she opened it, he handed her a cup of hot chocolate and a doughnut. "I thought this would tide us over until we get home."

"Thank you. I appreciate it." She smiled as he sat down across from her.

They quickly finished their breakfast and grabbed their luggage just as someone knocked on the door. Nick went to answer it. When he opened the door, the hotel manager was standing there.

"Dr. Creighton, I'm sorry to bother you, but there has been an accident. One of our guests just fell down the stairs. I called 911, but they said it will be a while before they can get here."

Nick grabbed his bag and followed the man down

the hall, with Abby close behind them. At the bottom of the staircase a man sat on the floor beside a young woman whose leg lay at an odd angle. They both appeared to be in their mid twenties. Even to Abby, who'd never had any medical training, it was obvious the woman's leg was broken.

Nick stooped down next to her. "This is Abby, and I'm Dr. Creighton. Looks like you took a pretty good fall."

She looked up at him. "This isn't a very nice way to end our honeymoon." Tears welled in her brown eyes. "I'm sorry, Kevin."

"Honey, it was an accident; you don't have anything to be sorry for. Dr. Creighton, I didn't want to try to move her. She fell from about midway up the stairs. I'm Kevin Standridge and this is my wife, Cindy."

"That was a wise decision. It's nice to meet you both, but I wish it were under different circumstances. Let's take a look at you, Cindy. Do you hurt anywhere besides your leg?"

"I hurt all over." She looked up at him. "But I think I'm just bruised. My leg is the only thing that really hurts. I'm sure it's broken."

"I could pretty well guess it is, but let's take a closer look. I'll try to be as gentle as I can."

When Nick touched her leg, she cried out. "I know that hurts. I'm sorry. It's definitely broken in at least two places. There isn't a lot I can do here. You need to go to the hospital to be X-rayed. Kevin, I don't want to move her." Nick turned to the hotel manager and asked if he could get them a pillow and blanket. He returned with it and Kevin placed the pillow under Cindy's head while Nick covered her with the blanket.

"Hopefully that will make you a little more comfortable until the ambulance gets here." Nick smiled sympathetically.

Abby prayed for Cindy as she gasped in pain when she tried to shift into a more comfortable position on the floor. "Cindy, I know the floor isn't very comfortable, but I'd be best if you try not to move until the ambulance gets here and they can get you to the hospital for X-rays."

From the looks of Cindy's leg, Abby knew she had to be in a lot of pain. In all of her twenty-two years, Abby had been fortunate never to have had a broken bone. Therefore, she didn't know from experience, but she could imagine how badly it had to hurt.

"Oh, I feel sick." Cindy placed her hand over her mouth as if she was going to vomit.

Abby ran to the counter. "Do you have anything she can use?"

The man at the counter handed her a plastic waste-basket. Abby ran back and handed it to Cindy, then went into the restroom and wet a couple of paper towels and took them to her.

"Thank you," she said just as she lost the contents of her stomach.

Kevin took the paper towels from Abby and bathed Cindy's face, all the while crooning lovingly to her.

"There's the ambulance." Nick said as sirens sounded from a distance. He explained Cindy's injury to the paramedics when they came in the door with a gurney.

Kevin shook Nick's hand. "Thank you, Dr. Creighton. We appreciate your help, and it was nice to meet you and Abby. I don't know how far you have to go, but it's nasty out there. We'll keep you in our prayers for a safe trip."

"I couldn't do much," Nick said. "But you'll be in our prayers, as well. Cindy, I wish you the best."

"Thank you," Cindy said as the paramedics wheeled her out the door with Kevin following.

Chapter 8

"Well, we've had a pretty exciting morning. I sure hope Cindy will be all right." Abby picked up her purse and overnight bag from the floor next to the stairway.

"It will take some time but I think she'll be okay. I hope her leg won't require surgery. I didn't feel any obvious splinters in the bone, but you never know for sure until you see the X-rays."

He was a good doctor. Abby was touched by his kind and caring attitude. "I'll keep them in my prayers. I'm glad she gave me her card with her e-mail address. I gave her mine, and she said she'd send me a note to let us know how she's doing. I feel for them. Cindy said they'd only been married a week. Fortunately, she said their honeymoon was over and they were leaving to go home. It would have been really awful if she had fallen on their first day." Abby glanced down at Cindy's business card. "Wow, it says on her card she's a Christian romance author. They aren't very far from Pierce City. They live in Springfield. What a story for a new book, huh?" She giggled as they went out the door and headed for the parking lot.

Nick chuckled. "Another author to add to your collection." He knew how she loved to read Christian romance. When they were together, she must have had more than a hundred books in her collection.

"Do you still have all of your books?" he asked as they climbed into the Blazer and closed the doors.

"Yes, I still have them, and I've added a few since I saw you last." She grinned and reached to fasten her seat belt. "I still collect my favorite authors. I went to the Christian section at the bookstore and bought their new ones before I left so I could bring them with me."

"You've read those same authors for a long time. I remember seeing their books on your shelves." Nick glanced over at her.

"Yes, I still have every book they've written in my bookcase at my apartment."

"Books and dolls—you always did love them." Nick smiled at her. "It's nice to have hobbies you enjoy."

Abby smiled to herself. Nick had always been tolerant of her love of books and dolls. Actually, he had always wanted her to have anything that made her happy. She knew that wasn't always true in every relationship. She had friends who weren't so fortunate. She had spent a long time in prayer last night before she went to sleep, asking the Lord to please help her to make the right decision about Nick, and she believed He'd given her an answer. He helped her to realize that Nick was everything she had ever wanted in a husband. She couldn't ask for a more dedicated Christian man; plus he shared her beliefs. After much soul searching, she decided she'd put her trust in Nick one more time.

"You're awfully quiet this morning. Are you okay?" Nick asked softly.

"Yes, I'm fine. I've just been thinking. I spent some time in prayer last night, and I've made some decisions." She looked at him, and tears filled her eyes. She blinked, and they spilled over, making a path to her chin. She wiped them away with the back of her hand. "I love you, Nick."

He pulled the car over to the side of the road and parked. As he turned, he drew her into his arms. "I love you, too, Abby, with every part of me. You are my life. I haven't been whole since the night we parted. If you can find it in your heart to forgive me and give me another chance, I promise I won't ever hurt you again."

"Through long hours of prayer as I lay awake last night and with the Lord's help, I came to the realization that under the circumstances with Janine, you made the only choice you could have made."

Nick's heart sang with happiness. He'd waited so long for this day. *Thank You, Lord*, he breathed silently as he kissed Abby, holding her close. He cupped her chin, gently lifting it where he could see her face. "I love you so much, Abby. I want to spend the rest of my life with you, doing everything I possibly can to make you happy. Would you be willing to move back to Pierce City? Will you marry me, be my wife, and be a mother to Scotty?"

His chest tightened as he waited anxiously for her to answer.

"Yes, I'll move back to Pierce City. I haven't truly been happy since I left. Just being with you will make me happy." She ran her fingers through his hair. "And yes, I'll marry you. I look forward to being your wife, and I'll do my best to be a good mother to Scotty."

He breathed a sigh of relief and gently squeezed her hand. "I have your ring in my safe at the house. We can go by and get it on the way to Granny's." He looked directly into her eyes for a moment. "Now I'd like to know why you won't play your guitar anymore."

She looked away. "Because it brought to mind too many hurtful memories. You loved to hear me play, and every time I picked up my guitar, I saw your face. The way you used to close your eyes and listen so intently when I'd play and sing—it broke my heart, so I put the guitar in Granny's bedroom closet and closed the door. It's still there."

"Abby, I'm so sorry." He placed a finger under her chin and turned her head toward him. "Will you play it again for me?"

She looked at him for a moment and then nodded.

"One more thing before we drive into town. You need to prepare yourself for what you're going to see. I know you saw all the coverage on the damage Pierce City suffered from the tornado. But watching it on television and seeing it in person is a totally different thing. The whole downtown was devastated. There wasn't much left standing. They're rebuilding, but it doesn't look anywhere near the same as it did when you left." Nick kissed her once more before he started the car and pulled back onto the highway.

They drove into Pierce City about an hour later. "Oh, Nick!" Abby cried, placing her hand over her mouth in shock. "I can't believe this. You weren't kidding when you said the tornado didn't leave much. It did so much damage." The devastation was incredible. Sadness washed over her. A few of the original buildings still standing had been repaired, but most of them were gone. She remembered the last Happy Neighbor Days gathering she had been to. She could close her eyes and picture it as it had been.

"It breaks my heart. Almost all of those quaint old buildings are gone now. But we're very fortunate there weren't more killed or injured, and that's the most important thing. The Lord really protected our families. Fortunately, they live three miles out in the country. They're far enough away from town that they weren't affected by the tornado, and for that I'm very thankful."

"I know, sweetheart." Nick sighed. "I am, too, and as you can see, they're rebuilding the downtown area. It won't be long now. They're almost finished. The businesses will soon be back up and functioning again. It will never be quite the same, but as close as they can make it. The love and closeness of the people in this town can never be destroyed, and that's what matters."

Abby smiled sadly as they drove the rest of the way through town on their way to Nick's house. So many memories flashed through her mind. She had grown up in this quaint little town.

"You're right, and I'm thankful to see they're almost done. I love this town and all of the people in it. I always have. It will always be my home."

Nick stopped in front of a set of gates and unlocked the chain holding them closed, then slid the gate open and got back into the Blazer. A few minutes later, he parked in front of a large Victorian-style house. She loved it. It was exactly what she would have built. It stood two stories tall with a wide front porch, and it was surrounded by trees. A large red barn almost as big as the house sat back and to the right side of the property. It was quite an impressive place. Since they were short on time Abby waited in the car while Nick went in to get her ring. But she intended to have a full tour of it when they had more time. Excitement at the thought of living in this beautiful place with Nick made her giddy. She wanted to get out and do a little dance around the yard. She refrained herself but just barely. Wouldn't that be a sight? She laughed.

Nick placed some Christmas packages in the trunk and then slid in beside her a few minutes later and started the car. As they drove back down the long driveway, Abby glanced behind her.

"I love your house. I can't wait to see the inside." She turned back around and refastened her seat belt. "It's so beautiful out here with all of these trees. I'll bet it's gorgeous in the springtime when all of their branches are filled with lush green leaves."

"It's our house, and it is beautiful in the spring. That's one of the reasons I built out here in the country. It was with you in mind. I prayed every night that one day soon you'd share it with me." Nick glanced over at her, a smile creasing his handsome face. He stopped to lock the gate and then headed toward Pierce City so the girls could have their traditional breakfast with Granny and hang the ornaments.

They drove up the long driveway, and just as they pulled up in front of Granny Forrester's house, Abby's cell phone rang.

Abby slid her phone out of the case and answered. "Hello?"

"Hi, Abby, this is Sandy. Remember me? We met in the women's restroom at the Denver airport."

"Sandy, I'm so glad to hear from you. How are you?"

"I'm just fine. I've moved in with my grandmother now, and she is going to help me with the baby. I wanted to call and tell you that I read the scriptures you gave me. Between reading them and talking to my grandmother, I've asked Jesus to come into my heart."

"Sandy that's wonderful. I'm so thrilled."

"I just want to thank you for caring enough to take the time for a lonely, devastated girl you didn't even know. You are a special person, Abby. Because of you, I have found Jesus and He has changed my life. Have a very nice Christmas, and I'll be in touch again soon."

"That's great, Sandy. I'm so happy for you. You have a Merry Christmas, too. I'll keep you in my prayers and look forward to hearing from you again." Abby hung up the phone and shared their conversation with Nick.

"That's fantastic, sweetheart. You just never know where the Lord is going to give you an opportunity to witness for Him. We need to always be ready for any opportunity He lays before us. A few short minutes in that airport bathroom and you helped lead a lost soul to Jesus." He smiled and wrapped his arm around Abby's shoulders as they walked up the steps that led to the wide front porch. Before they went in the door, Nick drew Abby into his arms and kissed her. "Can we sit on the swing for a minute before we go inside?" Nick asked.

"Sure." Abby walked across the porch with him, and they sat on the swing. Nick reached for her hand and slipped the engagement ring onto her left-hand ring finger. "Now it's back where it belongs." He smiled and kissed her forehead.

"I'd like for you to open this gift before you go in. The others I put in the trunk. I'll give them to you tonight when we have the traditional gathering around the tree." Nick handed her a small, brightly wrapped package.

Abby tore the paper and opened the box. "Oh, Nick!" she cried softly. "It's perfect. I love it." She grinned and lifted the Christmas ornament from the bed of cotton. "A wooden guitar. It looks exactly like mine." It had "Branson" with a date painted on the front. She looked up at him, confused. "Why does it have last year's date instead of this year?"

He smiled. "I bought it last year, along with the others. We were separated shortly afterward, and I never had a chance to give them to you. I kept them, praying I'd have another chance. I'm glad you like the ornament. I wanted you to have it to hang on the tree this morning."

"Thank you, Nick. I'll cherish it, and it will always be a special reminder of just how blessed we are to have another chance to be together."

Nick drew her to him again and kissed her. She loved the secure feeling of being held in his strong arms.

As they sat in the quiet, country atmosphere on her grandmother's porch, Abby realized that the Lord had brought her and Nick back together to raise a beautiful little boy and that He had gotten them home safely in time to spend Christmas with her family. He used the situation for her to witness to a devastated young girl, bringing Sandy into the family of God. The Lord certainly worked something good out of their suffering. Romans 8:28 came to mind: *"We know that all things work together for good to them that love God, to them who are the called according to his purpose."* Sitting there in Nick's arms, Abby prayed silently, thanking and praising the Lord for all of their blessings. She had made a Christmas wish, asking God to provide a way for her to be home for Christmas. Not only had He granted that request, but He had reunited her with Nick, her true love, her soul mate.

Jeanie Smith Cash

Jeanie lives in the country in Southwest Missouri, in the heart of the Ozarks, with her husband, Andy. They were blessed with two children, a son-in-law, and three grandchildren. When she's not writing, Jeanie loves to spend time with her family, spoil her grandchildren, read, collect dolls, crochet, and travel. Jeanie is a member of American Christian Fiction Writers. She loves to read Christian romance and believes a salvation message inside of a good story could possibly touch someone who wouldn't be reached in any other way.

Home for the Holidays

by Christine Lynxwiler

Dedication

This book is dedicated to my husband Kevin, who was first my best friend, then the love of my life. It's been a wonderful 25 years, honey. Here's hoping for many, many more together. Thank you for being the most supportive, encouraging hero a girl could ever have!

Special thanks to my sister and crit partner Jan Reynolds who read every word of this story umpteen times. Thanks also to Candice Speare and Rachel Hauck for great crits! And a great big thanks to my nephew Jeff and niece-in-law Lauren for letting me use your names. Y'all have something special. Praying many happy years ahead of you.

Chapter 1

Sure, Mrs. Whitfield. I'll be there in ten minutes." Lauren Forrester flipped her cell phone closed and slid it into her pocket. She turned her key in the lock of the Pierce City Library door and headed across the brightly lit parking lot to her car. Why was solving other people's problems so much easier than solving her own? The older woman, a regular at the library, depended on Lauren to take her to get groceries on Friday nights. Lauren didn't mind. At least she wasn't home moping. Or mopping, which was her other choice these days. Her apartment had never been cleaner.

Her best friend, Jeff, had been bugging her to tell him what was wrong, but she couldn't put a label on it. Restlessness? That wasn't really right. She had her suspicions, but even in the dark of her own bedroom when she poured out her heart to God, she wasn't ready to face the truth yet.

Before she could delve deeper into her apparently semi-warped psyche, she arrived at Mrs. Whitfield's little tin-roof house on the outskirts of town. Lauren quickly pulled out her tangerine-scented lotion and slathered it on her hands as she waited for the woman to come out. The lotion was her insurance against the elderly woman's hit-and-miss bath routine. Lauren could absently adjust her wire-rimmed glasses for a whiff of fresh tangerine if the odor was too bad.

A few minutes and several citrus inhalations later, Lauren dropped her passenger off in front of Town and Country. "Want me to come in with you?"

"No thank you, dear. When I get too old to buy my own groceries, they need to put me in a home. But that day's not here yet." Same answer every week.

Lauren smiled. "I'll be watching for you to come out."

She waited while the gray-haired woman shuffled through the automatic doors, then circled the lot to get a spot under a guard light so she could read her book. When she looked up from her story, the clock on the dash read nine o'clock. The library had stayed open until eight for a special Egyptian exhibit. Her friend and coworker, Becky, had a family to go home to, so Lauren had volunteered to work late.

The older woman should be done in a few minutes. And then what? Friday night and nothing to do except go home to her one-bedroom apartment over her parents' detached garage and clean the bathroom again. Lauren loved the small-town life, but she almost wished for the big city, a place where the sidewalks didn't roll up at nine.

The loud ring of her cell phone startled her out of her reverie. "Hello?"

"Hey, Laur. Meet me at the swings?"

"Jeff? What are you doing home this early on a Friday night?"

She'd known Jeffrey Warren so long she could almost hear the shrug.

"It didn't go so hot with Tina."

Big surprise. Why should Tina be any different than Jennifer or Mandy? Or any other girl in their singles group? "Give me half an hour."

"Half an hour? Since when does it take you more than five minutes to run down the stairs and across the field to the swings?"

She could feel a smug smile cross her lips. "For your information, I'm not home."

"Oh, that's right—the exhibit ran you late. You must be waiting for Mrs. W to get groceries."

The smile disappeared. How predictable could she get? "Yeah."

"You're too nice, Lauren."

"She needs me."

"Isn't there a service that would get her groceries for her?"

"We've been through this, Jeff. It's not the same thing. She feels independent this way."

He mumbled something she didn't catch. Sounded like "taking advantage," but she wasn't sure.

"I help her because I want to."

"I know. I hope none of your underdogs ever turns on you. See you after a while."

"See ya." She disconnected and jumped out to help Mrs. Whitfield with her groceries.

Twenty minutes later, Lauren hurried across the moonlit backyard, running her fingers through her shoulder-length hair. At times like this, her exasperating natural curls came in handy. Not that Jeff would notice if she spiked her dark brown hair and dyed it green. They didn't worry about looks with each other. Considering the old Show-Me-State sweatshirt and ragged jeans she'd hurriedly thrown on, it was a good thing.

When she neared the border of her parents' property, she stopped. The moon hung high, silhouetting the old swing set. How many times had they met there over the years? No one really knew where the swing set had come from. Maybe it had been there when Jeff's grandparents had bought the small white house on two acres. Or it could have been his mother's and his uncle's when they were young. Either way, it was Jeff and Lauren's now. Had been since they were ten.

Jeff, his broad shoulders framed in the moonlight, gave her a sheepish grin and rubbed his dark curls. "Hey."

He'd certainly changed since the first day she saw him. At ten years old, his deep blue eyes had seemed to fill his thin face when he told her that his grandparents had just adopted him. Later that night, she'd overheard her parents saying that Jeff's mother had overdosed and died. Hiding there on the stairs, Lauren had determined then not to let anything else bad happen to her new friend if she could help it.

"Hey, yourself. What happened with Tina?"

"I can't seem to get the whole dating thing right."

Lauren sank into a swing, sliding her grip down the coolness of the chains. "Then she's not the girl for you."

Jeff folded his muscular frame into the plastic swing and began pushing it back and forth with his foot. "Maybe it's just me, but tonight she chattered the whole time about her bridesmaid's dress for her sister's wedding. I also know what her sister's dress looks like, and I don't even *know* her sister. It was worse than that time you dragged me to the mall to help pick out a birthday present for your mom." He looped his elbow around the chain and waved his hand in the air as if brandishing an imaginary scarf. "But do you think this orange will clash with her hair?" His falsetto rang through the night stillness in sharp contrast to his normal deep voice.

Lauren snorted. "Dragged you to the mall, my foot. You had a coupon for free curly fries. And for your information, Mama's hair is auburn and that scarf was red."

He held up his hand. "You're not going to tell me about your mama's new dress, are you?"

She laughed. "You knew Tina talked a lot before you asked her out. Face it. You like the challenge of making a girl like you, but after that it's over for you. Look at how you are about Krista. You can't stand it that she's engaged. But if she weren't, you'd find something wrong with her." Every time they had the "there's nobody in the singles group for me" conversation, he'd bring up Krista as the example of someone who could have been the right one *if* she hadn't already been taken when she moved to Pierce City and joined their church singles group.

"Ouch. You know how to make a guy sound shallow, don't you?" He glanced over at her.

"Nah." She shook her head. "I know you're ready to settle down."

"But not with just anybody. It has to be the right girl."

The right girl. It didn't take a therapist to recognize that Jeff's strong desire to have a home and children was partly a result of living his first ten years with a self-absorbed drug addict who couldn't provide even his basic needs most of the time. "Let's see. Good with kids." She counted the words off on her fingers. "A sense of humor. Intelligent. Oh yeah, and don't forget blond, right? See? I know all your requirements—I should. I've heard them often enough." Did he know what *she* was looking for in a mate? For that matter, did she? Her heart seemed to have a mind of its own these days.

Back to the problem at hand. Time for a future-mate identity crisis later. "Jeff, there's someone out there for you. You just haven't found her yet." She couldn't think of one who could live up to his standards, but God must have someone special for a guy as great as Jeff. "Quit trying so hard. You've already broken the heart of every girl in Pierce City and all the neighboring towns. Pretty soon you'll have to go to Springfield or St. Louis to find someone."

"Can you see me with a city girl? I can imagine what would happen the first time I ordered frog legs."

"News flash. Even most small-town girls think frog

legs are gross, Jeff." She grinned. Leave it to him to bring it down to food. "Besides, all you have to do is show your dimples, and she'll forget about supper."

His laughing denial barely registered as she thought about her own words. How true they were. Maybe if relationships with the opposite sex hadn't come so easy to the ruggedly handsome contractor, he wouldn't be so picky. Even as choosy as he was, though, eventually he'd find that one special girl. And where would that leave his faithful sidekick and best friend since fourth grade? Taking Mrs. Whitfield to get groceries every Friday night? Or accepting a pity invitation from Jeff and his new wife for dinner once a week? A pang shot through her heart as the scene played out in her mind's eye.

She could imagine Jeff, his arm draped affectionately around a gorgeous blond, a delicious secret sparkling in their eyes. "Say hello to Aunt Lauren," Jeff would say and pat his wife's little round tummy. Lauren would smile and congratulate them, then spend the rest of the night watching Jeff treat the mother-to-be as if she were a precious piece of fragile crystal.

Lauren pushed off hard with her tennis shoe and clutched the chains as the swing soared up into the darkness. The cool wind rushed past her face, whispering secrets in her ears. For a minute, she allowed herself a glimpse of a different future. When she came back down to earth, she looked over at her best friend gliding lazily in the swing beside her. After years of being satisfied with friendship, why had her heart betrayed her now?

Jeff Warren had planned at least to be engaged by now. His twenty-fifth birthday had just passed, his carpentry business was going well, and his personal building project was almost done. He'd worked on it every spare minute for the last four years. Since Lauren had been back in town, she'd helped him on Saturdays, and the little details were coming together.

He wasn't unhappy living in his grandparents' small frame house. It was empty anyway since Grandma and Grandpa retired to Florida, and they were glad to have him around to take care of things. But this place. He looked across the front yard at the sparkle of the rolling river. This place was different. This was his dream house.

His future home. And someday, soon hopefully, when he finally found the woman "God had in mind for him," as Lauren always put it, it would be their home. He hammered the last board of the porch railing in place, then leaned against it. A crisp breeze off the water tickled his face. But the tall chain link fence around the property ensured that a small child wouldn't wander too far. The world was a dangerous place for a kid with no protection.

He closed his eyes and listened. A cricket chirped a greeting to a friend across the grass, and the tree frogs forecast an evening shower. In the distance the garrumphing croak of a bullfrog made him smile. Wouldn't it be wonderful to go to sleep listening to that as a child? A far cry from the roaring bus engines and screaming neighbors, or worse, his own mother's voice screeching at her latest druggie boyfriend.

He'd finally found peace.

The national anthem jarred him from his reverie. He snatched his cell from his belt and looked at the caller ID. "Hi, Laur, what's up?"

"I thought you'd be here by now."

He paused. Be where? Suddenly he remembered. The

singles group was meeting at the Taco Palace in Monett. He hit his forehead with the palm of his hand. He was supposed to pick Lauren up. When he'd finished his current job early, he'd only intended to spend a couple of hours working on his new house, but time had gotten away from him. "How about we meet there?"

Silence.

"Is that okay?"

"Oh. Okay. Sure."

"Listen, I'm running a little late and don't want you to have to wait."

"That's fine." She was using her bright smiley voice—like she did when she was hurt but trying not to show it. "I'll see you there."

What was her problem? "Lauren, wait—" He shook his head. Too late. She'd already broken the connection.

When he pulled into the Taco Palace parking lot, he looked at his watch. If Lauren had waited for him, she'd have been fifteen minutes late. Still, he felt a twinge of guilt. They'd made a pact to go to these things together because both of them were uncomfortable with the whole singles scene. Even though it was a church group, they felt less vulnerable together than alone.

Their friendship had been based on that foundation since they'd met. She'd helped him catch up in school, making up for time lost by being dragged from one seedy neighborhood to another, and in a small way, he'd returned the favor by protecting her from taunts of "brainiac" and "four eyes."

He spotted Lauren's bright red sweater immediately across the crowded restaurant. She always wore red when she was nervous. Said it gave her instant confidence. Guilt hit him again. Had she been wearing it before he'd stood her up?

Brad Lawton stood at the head of the table, and from his exaggerated hand motions, his story was a whopper. Everyone laughed.

Jeff walked up behind the medium-built blond man and clapped a hand on his shoulder. "Telling another fish story, Lawton?"

Brad grinned. "Had to do something to keep these women entertained. Thought you weren't going to make it." He and Jeff were two of the four men in the female-dominated group. Roger and Matt, the other two, were notoriously shy and barely responded when spoken to.

Choruses of "Hi, Jeff" came from around the table. He tried to catch Lauren's eyes to flash a silent apology, but she was talking to a couple of other girls.

"Hi." He started to take the empty seat next to her, but Brad slid into it before he did. The only other empty seat was between Tina and Krista, who was engaged to some guy in Indiana. He walked around and sat down. At least this would force Lauren to get over her mad spell. Seated straight across from him, she couldn't avoid his gaze all night.

"So, Jeff, Krista was just telling us that she and Ron broke off their engagement." Lauren smiled directly at him.

He floundered for words and looked at the gorgeous blond on his right. "Really?"

Lauren kicked him under the table as if to say, "Now's your chance. Don't blow it." Or knowing her, it could mean "Close your mouth. You look like a fish."

"Are you making it okay?" He looked at Krista, taken aback by her perfect beauty all over again.

She nodded. "I truly believe it's God's will. Things weren't working out with Ron, so He must have something better planned for both of us."

Her voice even sounded spiritual, innocent and childlike.

"Well, it's good that you found out now, I guess."

Krista smiled at him as if he'd said something brilliant. "Yes, I think so, too. But for a while I'm going to have to work to keep my mind off of it."

Jeff had some ideas about that. But asking someone out in a group setting just wasn't done. Maybe he could catch her afterward. He winked at Lauren across the table. She looked startled, then excused herself from the table. He hoped nothing was wrong with his best friend on this wonderful night. He'd have to tell her later that she'd hit the nail on the head with her prediction. The right girl had come along at just the right time.

Chapter 2

*W*ANTED*—C*HILDREN*'S L*IBRARIAN*:*
The St. Louis Public Library system seeks an energetic, upbeat individual who has experience working with children. Picture yourself as part of our dream team, where imagination, creativity, and knowledge are rewarded. The only requirements are flexibility, the ability to have fun, and an accredited MLIS.

When a girl unexpectedly falls in love with her best friend and he doesn't have a clue, distance is essential. Lauren double-checked her e-mail attachment, sent up a quick prayer, and hit SEND. The perfect job. Dealing with children, which she'd always loved. And most important, far away in the big city. Her résumé was on its way, and the rest, as her granny always said, was in the hands of the Lord.

She'd warned her parents and Granny of her intentions and asked them to pray, then tried to put the job application out of her mind. When the St. Louis Library called and set up a phone interview a few days later, she was stunned. The head librarian set her at ease immediately and seemed impressed with Lauren's answers to her questions. She called back to offer Lauren the job without even having her come to St. Louis to interview in person, and Lauren felt like her whole world tilted on its axis. Could she really do it?

Becky would miss her, but Lauren knew the busy mom needed more hours. She could move up to full-time now. They'd easily find someone part-time to fill Becky's old job. Obviously, God even thought she should get out of town.

Lauren's hand trembled as she dialed Jeff's cell number.

"Jeff Warren here." She knew by his impersonal greeting that he'd been too busy to look at the caller ID.

"Hi. It's me." She suddenly felt shy, which was ridiculous. This was Jeff, the boy who'd shared every detail of his life with her for umpteen years.

"Lauren, what's up?" His deep voice covered her like a warm blanket, giving her strength and comfort.

"Want to meet tonight and get a bite to eat?"

"Sure, I'd love to. Any special reason?"

"I've got some news." Keeping her tone neutral was easy because she had such mixed feelings.

"How about we make it lunch instead of supper? I'm not sure I want to wait to hear something that important."

Lauren looked at the clock. Thirty minutes until lunch. "I can do that."

"Good. I'll pick you up at twelve and we'll run down to Thompson's for a burger."

"You don't have to—"

"See you then."

He hung up before she could tell him she'd meet him there. She wondered if he noticed that she'd been avoiding being alone with him for the last few weeks. Ever since that night at the Taco Palace when Krista had announced she'd broken her engagement, Lauren had steered clear of personal conversation with Jeff. She'd seen him and Krista out together once, but they hadn't seen her.

As she thought of how she'd gone home and watched every old sad movie she owned that night, she knew the truth. If she stayed here, she'd ruin what was left of her and Jeff's friendship with her crazy infatuation. If she moved, she'd quickly forget those feelings and they could stay friends. *St. Louis, here I come. Now I just have to explain it to Jeff without him figuring out the truth.*

Half an hour later, she climbed into his shiny black pickup and smiled. In his red flannel shirt with the rolled-up sleeves revealing the cuffs of a thermal undershirt, he looked like he'd stepped off the pages of a men's catalog. "Hey."

"Hey, yourself. What's the mysterious news you couldn't tell me over the phone?"

She'd always loved Jeff's propensity to go straight to the point, but today she'd hoped for some time to get herself together. "Not mysterious really. You know how much I love working with children?"

He nodded but kept his eyes on the road.

"I've taken a children's librarian job in St. Louis."

He stomped on the brakes, and the truck squealed to a stop on the shoulder of the highway.

"Jeff! What are you doing?"

He looked at her. "What are *you* doing?"

A nervous giggle bubbled in her throat. "I'm moving to St. Louis."

"Why?"

How had she allowed herself to hope that question wouldn't come up? Her mouth suddenly felt so dry she couldn't speak. "It's a wonderful opportunity, Jeff."

His dark blue eyes seemed to be reading her most secret thoughts. She held his gaze, willing herself not to give anything away.

Finally, he looked back at the road. "I thought this was home to you."

She thought for a minute about the land she'd grown up on. Her grandparents had deeded twenty acres adjoining their farm to each of their four sons when they married. Lauren had grown up in the country, running and playing, skipping rocks, and flying kites with her cousins and then later with Jeff. "It is home. Always will be." A lump rose in her throat. "But trust me, Jeff. This move is what I need." She felt him looking at her again, and she forced herself to meet his eyes. "Okay?"

He stared at her, then grinned and pulled back onto the road. Was it her imagination, or did his smile look strained? "Okay. But I might as well buy stock in the oil companies. Think of how much gas I'll burn every time I need to talk to you in person."

"I'll be home for Christmas and a few days after. I made sure they'd give me a week off before I took the job. Besides, you won't need to talk to me as much since you're going out with Krista. How's that going, by the way?" She silently congratulated herself on both the smooth subject change and the casual tone.

"You'd know if you hadn't been so busy these last few weeks."

Ouch. So he had noticed she'd been avoiding him.

"I guess you had this secret in the works, so you didn't want to talk to me." He pulled into Thompson's packed parking lot and killed the engine. The hurt in his voice was as evident as it had been in ninth grade when she hadn't told him about her crush on Ricky Gray. When Jeff heard that Ricky was bragging he'd kissed Lauren, he'd been on his way to teach Ricky a lesson about lying when Lauren had intercepted him and admitted it was true. Of course, finding out Ricky was the type to kiss and tell had stopped that infatuation in its tracks. And Lauren had never really kept a secret from Jeff since then. Until now.

"I'm sorry. I was afraid you'd talk me out of it."

"I would have given it my best shot; I guarantee you that." He opened the door and looked over at her. "But if this is what you really want, I'll help you any way I can. It's the least I can do, as much as you've helped me."

She hated it when he acted like their friendship was one-sided because of where he'd come from. How many times had she told him that he'd given her as much as she'd given him? She opened her mouth to protest one more time, but before she could speak, he jumped out.

"Now, let's go get something to eat. Getting fired for being late back from lunch might make that big city library reconsider hiring you."

She climbed out of the truck and walked beside him to the door. Now that she faced the reality of being so far away from him, she almost wished the library *would* reconsider.

"What should I do with this, Jeffie?"

Did Krista try to sound like a little girl, or had her voice just never matured? Jeff cringed at the irritation surging through him. Lauren was right. He must be bound and determined to find something wrong with any girl he was dating. *Not this time, Laur. If you weren't moving halfway across the state, you could watch and see.* He shifted the stereo box he was carrying so he could see Krista, who was holding a mixer out away from her as if it were a dead cat. "Um, my guess would be in the box of kitchen stuff." He forced a smile.

"Oh. I guess that makes sense." She disappeared back into the den, but not for long he was sure. Krista, along with the rest of the singles, had come over to help Lauren pack things and load the truck and U-Haul trailer. But she was the only one who called him "Jeffie" and the only one who seemed to require his help with every item she picked up. He stomped out to place the stereo in the trailer. Sometimes he needed distance from his perfect girl.

The work went fast with everyone helping, and it wasn't long before he and Lauren stood in the doorway of her empty apartment and waved good-bye to the singles group. She'd said her good-byes to her family that morning, and her dad had taken her mom and her granny for a day trip to Branson. They'd all agreed it would be easier that way. Jeff had assured them that he would make sure Lauren got settled in her St. Louis apartment safely. He'd even loaded her car on a tow dolly behind the moving trailer so she could ride with him in his truck.

"Well, *Jeffie*," Lauren said with a wry grin, "are you ready to hit the road?"

He raised an eyebrow. Two could play the hated nickname game. "Sure am, Mutt. How about you?" Everyone in town had called them Mutt and Jeff until Lauren had hit her teenage years and had developed an aversion to being called Mutt. He dodged as she swatted at him. "Can't believe you're splitting up the team."

She spun around and walked through the tiny apartment. "It looks like we've got everything," she called back to him. "I'll be ready in a minute."

He heard the bathroom door close, and in a few minutes she came out, drying her face on a paper towel. "You okay?"

"Oh yeah, just grimy from all that packing. Thought I'd wash up." She wadded the paper towel into a ball with her clenched fist and brushed past him.

Right. Without a speck of makeup and her hair pulled up in a high ponytail, she looked about sixteen. And if he wasn't mistaken, she'd been crying. He was surprised by a sudden urge to keep her close and protect her. Instinctively he pulled up the mental boundary he kept between them.

Lauren had no idea, but in high school he'd come close to falling for her. His grandpa had realized it somehow. He'd taken Jeff aside for a man-to-man talk and explained the concept of "us" and "them." Sure, he'd said, the Forresters were good folk and friendly. But Jeff's grandpa would always be a hired hand to them. And Jeff would always be a drug addict's son and a hired hand's grandson.

Jeff argued that Lauren wasn't like that, but his grandpa had pointed out all the less fortunate people

Lauren helped, even back then. Suddenly, Jeff knew that in spite of their undeniable bond, he would always be an ongoing "project" to her. And she would always be his best friend, but never more than that. Someday he'd find a woman who loved him for himself, not out of pity. He thought of Krista, blond and perfect. Who knew? Maybe he already had.

He looked across the truck cab at Lauren, so confident-looking in her bright red sweatshirt. "You scared?"

She flashed him a glance. "A little."

"Me, too."

She snorted. "Silly goose. You don't have to stay there and live. All you have to do is drive me there."

And leave you there. Even though her place in his heart was clearly defined, it was still going to be hard to make it without her. "Yeah."

She shot him a puzzled look.

"What? St. Louis is a big city. I might get us lost." He raised an eyebrow. "Truth is, Lauren, I hate to see you go."

"We'll still be friends. It'll just be different. We've grown up, and things are bound to change. One of us will end up getting married before too long. Nothing lasts forever, Jeff."

Wasn't she Miss Polly Platitude? He guided the truck and trailer through town and onto the interstate. If he didn't know better, he'd think his best friend was dumping him.

Chapter 3

Do you want to check out that book, Brian?" Lauren asked.

"Yes, miss, if that's okay." The boy's jacket was threadbare and his jeans stained, but his blue eyes gleamed with subdued intelligence beneath his too-long bangs. Lauren had been trying to gain his trust for the past two months, but he still called her just "miss."

Lauren took the worn copy of *The Lion, the Witch, and the Wardrobe* from his hand and stroked it lovingly. "This is one of my favorites. Have you read it before?"

"No, ma'am."

"You'll have to let me know what you think."

"I will if I can." He pushed his dirty blond hair back from his face.

Over the past couple of weeks, Brian had grown more furtive and withdrawn, and for the hundredth time Lauren wondered what burdens those small shoulders were carrying. He showed up every day after school, did his homework at a table in the corner, then left right before closing time. On Saturdays, he stayed for hours. Did his parents care where he was? Did they allow him to wander the streets of the city without supervision?

"What do you mean?"

"I might have to drop it in the night box," he mumbled as she handed him the book back.

"Oh? Are you going somewhere for Christmas vacation?" It was still two weeks before the schools let out for the holidays. "Or are you moving?"

He looked up at her, as if measuring her trustworthiness. "I'm not sure." He clutched the book in his hand. "I've got to go."

Lauren looked out the window. Sheets of rain made it impossible to see the street outside. "Why don't you wait a few minutes until the rain lets up? Want me to call home for you?"

"No!" He shrugged his backpack onto the table and sank into a chair. "I'll wait. But you don't have to call."

Twenty minutes later when Lauren was about to leave, she noticed he was still sitting there staring at the rivers of water running down the window. "Brian, how far away do you live?"

He jumped at the sound of her voice. "Why?"

"I have a supersize umbrella," she said with a grin. "Big enough for both of us. I could walk you to your house." She'd been blessed to get an apartment less than a block from the library branch she worked at. Surely he didn't come from very much farther than that every day.

"No, thanks!" He grabbed his backpack and darted out the door ahead of her, heedless of his gloves falling to the floor.

She snatched them up and popped her umbrella open. The cold rain took her breath away as she hurried outside. "Brian, wait! You're going to catch your death." She broke into a sprint. Whatever was going on with him, he had no business out in this weather.

She finally caught up with him as he slid open the side door of a battered white minivan. The rain had slacked up enough for her to see there were no seats, only blankets and pillows. Brian climbed in and spoke to the driver, a woman. As Lauren stood there on the wet sidewalk clutching his worn gloves, the van sputtered away from the curb and disappeared into traffic.

Why hadn't Brian wanted her to walk him to his vehicle? Were they living in the van? Lauren's heart squeezed at the possibilities. Then she scolded herself for being so silly. He probably thought he was too tough to be seen riding with his mom. Who knew with boys that age?

As she turned to walk the short distance to her apartment, her cell phone rang and she glanced at the caller ID. Jeff again. For that matter, who knew with boys of *any* age? She'd been ignoring most of Jeff's calls and e-mails. Probably not the most mature decision she'd ever made, but she missed him so badly that talking casually with him felt like pouring alcohol on an open wound.

Her two-bedroom apartment echoed with her footsteps as she padded from room to room, throwing together a grilled cheese sandwich and a salad, eating alone, then getting ready for bed. She picked up her cell. One missed call. Maybe she'd sleep better if she called him. Her finger poised over the keypad. She could find out how the house was coming along. How their friends were doing. How things were going with Krista. She gave the END button a vicious jab and tossed the phone on her nightstand. She could go to sleep fine without talking to him. Eventually.

The next morning Lauren wondered if she'd made the right decision. The dark circles under her eyes seemed determined to defeat her concealer. No matter how much she put on, they reappeared like magic. When Brian didn't show up in the juvenile section that afternoon, worry kept her awake again. A week later she was going through the motions, going to work, coming home. She missed Jeff more than she wanted to admit. And now she couldn't get Brian out of her mind. Why hadn't she beat on the van door when she'd seen the blankets and pillows and asked his mom if there was anything she could do to help? She wondered where he was spending his afternoons.

On Monday she had to run an errand to the reference section. There, huddled in a chair in the corner, devouring an encyclopedia article with his intelligent eyes, was Brian. He jumped when he saw her but quickly turned his attention back to the text.

"Fancy meeting you here," she drawled softly.

He looked at her as if she were speaking a foreign language, and she took that as an invitation to sit down. Slowly. No sudden moves. "Everything okay?"

He stared at her, and for a minute she thought the dam might break and all the information he was holding back would flow forth with no restraint. But he just nodded.

She bent toward him and dropped her voice even lower. "Are you afraid I'll tell someone you live in the van?"

His eyelids opened wide. "We don't *live*"—he spat out the word, as if disgusted she could think such a thing—"in the van. We have a house." He stuck out his chin. "We own our own house."

Lauren felt heat rush to her cheeks. She'd done it again. Jumped to conclusions and embarrassed herself.

"We stay in the van some to get warm," he mumbled.

"You and your mom?"

He nodded.

"Because your house is cold?" Heating bills were high this time of year. But was gasoline cheaper?

He nodded again. "Our roof has big holes in it."

"Oh no."

"I gotta go."

"Wait, Brian." Her heart thudded. Would he run off again and never reappear this time? She prayed that God would keep that from happening as well as let her figure out the best way to help the boy and his mother. "I'm not going to tell anyone. I just want to help."

As if he read her mind, he said, "That's okay, miss. Mama says God will help us."

Lauren blinked back the tears that threatened to overflow down her cheeks. Nothing made boys more uncomfortable than overemotional girls. Even grown-up girls. "She's right. But I have some ideas about how He might do that. Can I talk to your mom?"

"I'll ask her tonight, and if she says yes, I'll bring her with me tomorrow."

"Is she at work?"

He ducked his head and mumbled.

"I didn't hear you."

"She had to quit. It's too close to time for the baby to come."

Lauren's heart froze in her chest.

"Not coming home at all?" Jeff stared at Lauren's grandmother. "Did she say why?"

Granny shook her head. "Not really. Just that some things had come up and she wouldn't make it for Christmas."

Jeff cleared his throat, but it still felt like a golf ball was lodged there. "Did she say anything about me? I haven't been able to get in touch with her lately."

"As a matter of fact, she said to tell you Merry Christmas." The old woman patted his hand and pushed to her feet. "Oh, and she mentioned there might be someone special you wanted to invite for our Christmas Eve get-together." Her faded brown eyes twinkled. "You know any friend of yours is always welcome here, Jeff. You're part of our family."

"Thanks. That means a lot to me." He'd always been at the Forresters' on Christmas Eve. But always with Lauren. He couldn't imagine coming without her.

As far as bringing someone, Krista was going home to Indiana for Christmas. With any luck, she'd work things out with her ex-fiancé. Jeff had been serving more as a counselor to her lately than anything else.

She called him frequently for a man's take on what Ron was thinking. And that was fine with him. She was a nice girl, but her baby voice and constant worrying about her looks drove him over the edge.

Jeff clutched his coffee mug. He'd stopped by to check on Granny, but they both knew that he really wanted news of Lauren. And now he'd gotten it. Suddenly, the frustration of the past couple of months boiled up inside him. He clunked his mug down on the table and stood. "I'm going to St. Louis."

Granny looked up from where she was washing her own cup at the sink. "What about work?"

Odd that she hadn't asked him why he was going. "We finished up the Johnson job today, and I gave the guys their Christmas bonuses. I'd allowed a month off for the holidays until we start the next house. I had planned to work out at my place." He hugged the older woman and dropped a peck on her cheek. "But first I've got to make sure Lauren's okay."

Granny's smile wreathed her face in wrinkles. "That's my boy."

Jeff laughed aloud at the exuberance coursing through him since he decided to take action. "I'll see you Christmas Eve. And hopefully I won't be alone!"

Two hours later, he was St. Louis bound. He prayed the whole trip. Lauren was tenderhearted, but she was also stubborn. If she had some harebrained idea about proving her independence in the big city by cutting off communication with her best friend, there was no guarantee he could change her mind. But he was going to give it his best shot.

As he walked up the stairs to her apartment, his heart thudded in his chest like a teenager's on his first date. What would she say? Would she slam the door in his face?

He knocked and waited.

After a few minutes, he heard footsteps, then a muffled, "Who is it?"

"Lauren, it's Jeff."

The door cracked open, and a boy peeked around at him. "She's not home right now."

"Brian? Who's at the door?" Jeff heard a female voice ask.

"Just a minute." The boy who looked to be about nine or ten closed the door. Jeff heard the lock click.

He pounded on the door. Was someone holding

Lauren hostage? What was going on?

"Jeff?"

He spun around. Lauren stood at the top of the stairs, two bags of groceries in her hands.

"Hey!" He stepped forward and took the plastic sacks. "Who are those people in your apartment?"

"What are you doing here?"

"Your granny said you weren't coming home for Christmas, so I came to check on you."

"You drove all the way here?" Her voice was incredulous. "Why didn't you just ca—" Her face flamed. "Oh."

"Yeah," he said wryly, "I did think of that, but I seem to have some difficulty getting through."

"Jeff." Lauren slid her key into the lock. "I'm sorry. I've been really busy here."

"I see that. Are you sharing an apartment now with someone from work?"

"Not exactly. Their house has some damage to the roof. They were living in their van. . ."

Jeff shook his head, his heart pounding as the truth of what she was saying hit him. "Tell me you didn't really invite homeless people to live with you." He slammed his hand against his leg. "Have you lost your mind?" At least in Pierce City the people she insisted on helping were harmless. But in the city, con artists ate girls like Lauren for lunch.

"Could you keep your voice down?" Lauren nodded toward the door.

"Oh yeah. Wouldn't want to offend the people who are taking shameless advantage of you." Jeff couldn't stop the sarcasm. He felt his face growing hot. "You've pulled some good ones, Lauren. But this one takes the cake."

Tears sprung to her eyes, and he knew he'd gone too far. Still, the thought of people like his mother getting their claws into someone as innocent and trusting as Lauren made it impossible for him to be civil.

"I understand that you're upset, Jeff, but I think you'd better go. Why don't you call me tomorrow?" She turned the knob and slipped into the apartment, closing the door firmly behind her. Jeff stared at the smooth white door. This wasn't how he'd envisioned their reunion.

Chapter 4

How dare he? Lauren shoved her hair out of her eyes and scrubbed at the tiny spot on the bathroom floor. He had no right to tell her what to do. She'd moved here to get away from him. She should have told him that. But then he'd have realized the truth. And that was the last thing she wanted.

Her cell phone hadn't stopped ringing since she'd closed the door on Jeff. She'd turned it on vibrate so it wouldn't disturb Connie. With the baby due in less than two weeks, Lauren's new friend wasn't getting much rest these days. She and Brian had gone to bed early. Lauren glared at the phone dancing across the bathroom counter. Did Jeff care about that? No, apparently not.

She paused mid-scrub and wiped away a tear with the back of her hand. *Lord, please help me to understand Jeff. And give me the courage to be his friend again. Even though I can't have the relationship I want to have with him, I don't want to lose him. Please.*

When she finished her prayer, she remembered something her mother told her long ago. She'd been twelve and reeling from the sudden death of her beloved dog, Copper.

"Lauren," her mother had said, "you love God now and you believe in Jesus, but when you go through trials, that's when your faith becomes your own." Lauren remembered thinking that if growing faith had to hurt as badly as this, she'd be happy depending on what her mom and dad believed for the rest of her life.

But her mother had been right. The past couple of months had been empty in many respects, yet Lauren had grown closer to God. He'd kept her from giving up, from turning away from others in her despair. She was grateful.

She stood and rinsed out her scrub brush. Because of his mother's manipulative nature, Jeff had never been overly compassionate to those in need. But he'd never openly opposed Lauren's desire to help others. He'd even helped her sometimes. She knew from Granny's letters that he was taking Mrs. Whitfield to get groceries every week. Suddenly, an idea so outrageous that it had to work popped into her mind. Jeff's presence here wasn't an irritant. It was a blessing. An answered prayer, even.

The doorbell rang, and Lauren hurried to the door. She'd let him in and explain the situation to him with patience and understanding. Then she'd beg him to help. She automatically glanced through the peephole, and her hand froze on the knob. A pizza man stood in the hallway with a square cardboard box clutched in his hands.

"Can I help you?"

"Pizza delivery."

"I didn't—" Before she could finish, he interrupted.

"For Lauren Forrester courtesy of Jeff Warren. He says it's your favorite."

Pepperoni and anchovies? Oh, he knew how to break

her down, didn't he? She groaned and opened the door. As the man handed her the pizza, she looked over his shoulder, half expecting Jeff to be lurking behind him, waiting to push his way in. But the hallway was empty. She didn't know if she was disappointed or relieved.

Pepperoni and anchovy pizza had been her favorite late-night snack when she was in college, but once she'd moved back to the country, she'd had to give it up. How many nights had she grumbled to Jeff that she'd love to have it again? Sneak. Trying to soften her up with food. Lucky for him she wanted to make up as much as he did.

She walked into the kitchen and plunked the steaming box down on the table. No need to let it go to waste. She grabbed a paper towel and flipped open the lid. A note in Jeff's handwriting was carefully taped inside the top flap of the box.

Dear Lauren,

I'm so sorry. It's none of my business what you do, but I want you to be safe. I promise not to discuss your guests if you will talk to me. Please.

Yours,

Jeff

She smiled. Leave it to him to cut to the heart of the matter. She picked up her phone and punched in his number. He answered on the first ring.

"Hey," he said. "Meet me at the swings?"

"Huh?" She glanced out the window at the apartment complex playground below. Jeff, folded into a swing three sizes too small for him, lifted his hand in greeting.

"I'll be right down."

"Bring the pizza."

"I should have known you just wanted me for my food." As soon as she said it, she wished it back. The silly words sounded too much like banter between a couple in love.

She didn't wait for a reply. But just as she pushed END, she thought she heard him murmur, "Not hardly."

Her heart skipped a beat. What did he mean by that?

Jeff pulled his denim jacket tightly around him and stared at the entrance to the brownstone apartment building. What was he going to say to her now that he'd coaxed her out? Before he could decide, she appeared at the door. He took the pizza box from her and set it on the picnic table. "Thanks for agreeing to see me. I'm sorry about awhile ago."

"Actually, I owe you an apology." Her voice trembled, and she looked about twelve. "For not taking your calls or being in touch. I—" She scuffed at the gravel with her toe.

"I know why you did that, Lauren." It had all become clear to him this afternoon when she'd stormed into her apartment.

She jerked her head up and stared at him, her eyes wide. "You do?"

He nodded. "Sure. I always thought I was looking out for you. But to you it must have seemed like I was treating you like a child. No wonder you were in such a hurry to move."

"No, Jeff. I didn't—it wasn't—" She grabbed the pizza box. "I can't think on an empty stomach. Let's discuss this later, okay?"

"Okay." He'd never understand women, but at least she didn't still seem to be mad at him. And he knew that was a good thing.

She sat at the picnic table and patted the seat beside

her. "Actually, even though you promised not to in your very sweet note"—her eyes sparkled as she smiled up at him—"I want to talk about my houseguests."

"I'd recognize that 'Oh, Jeff. I've got a plan' look anywhere, so you go ahead." He shot her a wry grin. "I'll listen."

"Did you see Connie earlier? Or just Brian?"

"Just the boy."

"His name's Brian, and he reminds me so much of you when you were that age."

"His mama a druggie?"

She frowned. "No! Connie's a sweet Christian woman with tremendous faith."

"That's what she wants you to think, Lauren." Where had that come from? He'd been biting his lip, but the words had slipped out anyway. "Sorry. Forget I said that."

Lauren's tiny hand covered his, and the cool night grew warmer. "I understand how you feel, Jeff. But she's just a woman like me, only she ended up in a bad situation."

He squeezed her hand. "I've got news for you. There aren't any other women like you." She cared so deeply about everything and everybody that it scared him. That quality kept him off guard, always made him afraid he would read too much into her affection for him.

"Good thing, huh? The world probably couldn't stand very many of me." She laughed. "Nice try at distracting me, but back to my story. Connie's husband is in prison. He *was* on drugs, and one day when he was visiting a friend's meth lab, the police showed up for a visit."

"Good for them," Jeff muttered around a big bite of pizza.

"Yes." Lauren leveled a steady gaze at him. "Good for them. And good for him, too. While he was incarcerated, he became a Christian. He was so excited about his new faith, that in one family visit, with some help from a prison ministry worker, he converted Connie and Brian, too."

Jeff stopped with his pizza slice halfway to his mouth. He'd always thought prison conversions were staged to look good at parole hearings, but if the man had taught his wife and son about Jesus, too. . . Of course, they could all be bluffing. "How long ago was that?"

"About seven months. He hadn't been in prison long when Connie found out she was pregnant."

"And they had nowhere to live?" Jeff hazarded a

guess, unsure whether he was buying this story or not.

"They own a small house in a neighborhood downtown, but after he got on the drugs, the roof started leaking, and he didn't fix it."

"Typical."

"Part of the roof caved in last month. Doug's supposed to get out right away, but what about in the meantime? When I met Brian, they were staying in the van most of the time trying to keep warm. He spent the afternoons at the library for a change of pace. Connie had lost her waitress job because she couldn't stay on her feet. What was I supposed to do?" Love and compassion shone in her eyes.

What indeed? Lauren had no choice but to love people. It was who she was. And when she loved, she loved with her whole heart. "Just what you did, I guess." He cleared his throat. "You know, I remember what it was like when my mother was alive."

She waited.

"The crowd she ran with would use anything to get to people. They weren't above using their kids." He frowned at the memories flooding his mind. "Or even their pregnancies." He dropped the slice of pizza, forcing down the bite in his mouth that suddenly tasted like sawdust. "They—we would be Christians of any variety. One Sunday we'd hit the Baptist church for a handout. The next week it would be time to be Methodist. One year I went to five different vacation Bible schools." Shame pushed the words out of his mouth. "She made me wear the most raggedy clothes I had so people would feel sorry for us. There was nothing she and her friends wouldn't do for a fix. And that included getting religion."

Tears splashed down Lauren's face, and she put down her own pizza. "That must have been awful."

"It took a couple of years of living with Grandpa and Grandma—and hanging around you and your family—before I realized how unchanging true faith was."

"You sure know what it is now. Your whole life shows that."

If only she knew how far from the truth that was. How the bitterness rolled up in his throat like acid when he thought of his mother and his life in the city. "Why are you trying to butter me up?"

"I'm not!" she said with mock indignation. "But I do have a favor to ask."

Jeff would walk across hot coals for her, but he had a feeling this "favor" was going to be a doozy. "What's that?"

"Connie's roof. I have some money left from what Granny gave me when I graduated college. I'd like to use it to buy shingles and supplies."

"You want me to help you pick out the right things? Shouldn't you let the roofer handle that?"

She cleared her throat and tilted her head to one side, keeping her eyes fixed on his. "I only have enough money for the materials."

"Then who's going to—" Realization dawned on him before he could finish his question. He should have hightailed it out of town without looking back as soon as she said the word *favor*.

Chapter 5

Lauren stacked another book back onto the rolling cart and sighed. Only four days until Christmas Eve. Granny would have fresh greenery and sparkling lights throughout the house. Her cousins would be making their last-minute travel plans. Her parents would be plotting and planning Santa Claus surprises for the local kids.

She wondered if Mama was making her famous cheese logs this year. Or if Daddy had strung lights on the big red barn. She'd have to call and ask. One year, she and Jeff had spelled out "Santa, stop here!" with lights on the barn roof. People from all over the county had driven by to see it. Christmas was Lauren's favorite time of year, but this year she wouldn't be a part of the two-week-long celebration on Forrester Farms. How had she thought she could stand to miss it?

Only the thought of facing Jeff had kept her away, and now he was in the city with her. He'd leave day after tomorrow to go home, in time for Christmas Eve at Granny's. But she would have to stay. There was no way she could leave Connie and Brian alone with the baby coming. And Connie definitely couldn't travel. Lauren blinked back hot tears.

A gray-haired man stopped beside her. "Excuse me, ma'am. Can you tell me where the books on vampires are?"

She directed him and turned back to the cart. She'd never seen him before. In Pierce City, she knew the library patrons by name. By the kind of books they preferred, even.

Take Thomas Maderro, for example. By day, he worked on the factory assembly line, but by night, he read cookbooks. Every variety he could find. Sometimes he'd bring in a plate of pastries for Lauren to try, other times, a nice casserole for Mrs. Whitfield. Whenever Lauren got a new cookbook in at the library, she always called to let him know. Did Becky do that for him now?

Mrs. Whitfield loved to pretend she was Miss Marple. She doted on mysteries. Lauren often noticed her watching the local residents with a suspicious eye, no doubt wondering who might have murder in his heart.

And little Samuel Evins. He read everything he could get his hands on and had since he was four. Brian reminded her of him, only Samuel had never missed a meal or gone to bed without a good-night kiss from his daddy.

She continued through the list of regulars in her mind, and by closing time she was so homesick she felt like she couldn't stay away another day. Funny thing, it wasn't even each individual person. It was the small-town life. The charming parts like the town square at Christmastime and the not-so-charming parts, like everyone knowing everyone else's business. She missed it all. Maybe she wasn't cut out to be a big-city girl.

She pushed open the double doors and stepped out into the frigid air. A bearded man with multiple face piercings bumped into her and kept walking without a word. On his bare right arm, a tattoo of a spider in a bikini belly-danced with the movement of his muscle. *Oh, Toto,* Lauren thought, *we're not in Kansas anymore.*

She ducked her head against the wind and concentrated on putting one foot in front of another. When her phone rang, she flipped it open with a grin. Jeff was right on schedule. "Hi, there."

"Lauren? Is that you?" In spite of the puzzled tone, Lauren recognized the voice of her old coworker Becky.

"Becky? What's wrong?" They were friendly but not close enough to call each other on a regular basis.

"Nothing's wrong. Something's right, actually. I'm pregnant."

"Congratulations! How wonderful." After Beth was born, Becky and Dan had wanted one more child, but Beth was ten now, and they'd just about given up. "I know you're excited."

"I sure am. But I'm going back to part-time. Before we advertised the full-time position, I wanted to be sure you were happy there."

"Oh." Was she happy here? It was a beautiful city, friendly people, pepperoni and anchovy pizza anytime, day or night. But it wasn't home. "Becky?" Lauren cleared her throat, but the lump stayed. "Can you give me a couple of days to think about it?"

"Sure! I'll hold the job until right after Christmas. Just let me know."

Lauren walked the rest of the way to the apartment in a daze. Why had she exiled herself like a criminal? Her only crime had been falling in love with the wrong man. Would it be so awful if she never married and went to eat with Jeff and his wife on Friday nights? Okay, that last part would be pretty awful. But staying single wouldn't be so bad. She might have to give up Jeff as a friend when he married, but at least she'd be doing it in the comfort of her own home, with her family nearby.

By the time she unlocked her door, she'd decided. She might not be able to get to Granny's for Christmas because of Connie and Brian, but after the baby was born and they were settled in, she was going to do more than visit. She was moving home.

By the next afternoon, Jeff knew without a doubt why he always tried to take a month off from mid-December to mid-January. This time of year, unless a man sported a red suit and a white beard while driving a sleigh pulled by reindeer, he definitely didn't belong up on a rooftop. A roaring fire would be more like it, along with a hot cup of coffee and a good book. Even an exasperating conversation with Lauren would beat trying to hold a shingle straight with frozen fingers.

He sat back on his legs and surveyed his work. He'd used over a bundle of shingles, and the job didn't look half bad if he did say so himself. Break time. He climbed carefully down the ladder and grabbed his coffee thermos. He might not be able to relax by the fire with a book, but he could drink coffee and call Lauren. She should be home from work now, and she'd been really worried about Connie the last time he talked to her. The doctors said it should be a few more days, but if there was one thing Lauren and Jeff knew from growing up on a farm, it was that babies came when they got good and ready.

He punched in Lauren's cell number and smiled. Now that he was in town, she'd gone back to accepting his calls. He still didn't know what that had been all about. But he was glad she was over it.

"Hello?"

"Hey, Laur. Everything okay?"

"Yes, unless you count Connie and Brian beating me at Monopoly."

"You're playing board games? I don't believe it! I'm stuck out here in the freezing cold, and you're all nice and cozy having the time of your life."

She chuckled and spoke softly. "Suck it up, you big baby. I'm not doing this for fun. I want to keep Connie's mind off these pains the doctor is calling false labor."

"You sound like you're not buying that assessment."

"I'm no expert, but it looks like the real thing to me, even if it is two weeks until her due date." He could hear the worry in her voice. "How bad is the roof?"

"Not as bad as it could be. I think I can have it done in a day and a half."

"That's wonderful, Jeff. Thank you so much," she whispered. They had planned to surprise Connie and Brian with the new roof.

"Hey, do you feel like having Chinese takeout for supper? I can pick some up after I stop by the hotel and shower."

"I know you're tired. Will you feel like it?"

"I can't think of anything I'd rather do." As Jeff said

the words, he realized how true they were. Why was he in such a hurry to find his perfect girl? He could have a good time hanging out with Lauren and being single. Then when the right woman came along, he'd be ready, but it wouldn't be something he'd rushed into.

"Thanks, Jeff. I appreciate you so much. You're a lifesaver."

He dropped the phone back in his pocket. A throat cleared behind him. He spun around to face a tall, gangly stranger.

"Can I help you?"

The man ran his thumb across the bill of the grease-stained cap he held between his hands. Even though he didn't look to be over thirty, he appeared to have lived a lifetime already, and the solemn expression in his eyes reminded Jeff of someone. "Actually, I was hoping I could help you."

"I'm sorry, buddy," Jeff said and realized he really was sorry. He'd like to help someone out without Lauren's prompting. "This is a volunteer job, so I can't afford to hire any help." Plus, his worker's comp probably wouldn't cover an indigent worker he hired in St. Louis—but no need to go into that.

"I don't need any money. Just want to help." The man's Adam's apple bobbed as he seemed to be weighing his words.

Jeff frowned. What kind of scam was this? He must be losing his mind. For a minute, he'd suckered right into the man's sincere-seeming demeanor and softly spoken words. "Thanks, but no thanks."

He walked away, hoping the con artist would take the hint, but the man hefted a pack of shingles onto his shoulder and started up the ladder.

"Hold it right there. I'm going to have to call the cops if you don't come down."

The man paused on the first step of the ladder. "The cops can't run me off."

Jeff stared in horror as the bum tossed the bundle of shingles to the ground with a thud and reached inside his right jacket pocket.

"And neither can you."

Chapter 6

Jeff jumped back and started to dive behind his truck.

"Whoa, man." The man held up a battered wallet. "Just showing you some ID. I live here."

"Says who?"

"Says the deed to the house and this identification." He stepped down and stuck out his hand. "I'm Doug Miller. I should have introduced myself, but when I saw you working here, I thought you must know Connie, and I was still figuring on surprising her."

"You're Connie's husband?" Jeff shook his hand as he suddenly realized who Doug looked like. He was a grown-up version of Brian. "I thought you were—" He stopped, unsure what to say.

"In prison? I was." Doug's soft smile took years off his age. "Up to a couple of days ago. Rick Watson down at Rick's Auto Shop teaches a Bible class at the prison, and when I got out, he took me on as a mechanic. I wanted to work a few days and get enough to start fixing the house up before I told Connie and Brian the good news." He shook his head. "It's hard not to rush to see her, though."

"I can imagine." Jeff found himself liking this man in spite of his history. Would his mom have been this nice if she'd ever gone straight? Who knew? "I'm a friend of Connie's friend, Lauren."

"Really? Lauren's an amazing person, the way she's taken Connie and Brian into her home. Most people wouldn't do a thing like that." Doug took off his cap again and clutched it.

"Lauren's one of a kind," Jeff agreed. "Have you talked to Connie lately?"

"We talk every Friday. I was hoping to be able to surprise her and Brian in person this Friday." He looked at the sunset and the darkening clouds. "Guess today's a bust. But tomorrow's my day off. I can help you all day." He chuckled. "I'm no roofer, so you'll have to tell me what to do."

Jeff clapped him on the back. "Get a good night's rest. With both of us working, we may get the roof done tomorrow."

An hour later, Jeff hurried into the brownstone, clutching a bag full of Chinese food. He hadn't known what Brian and Connie liked, so he'd gotten a variety. He decided not to mention Doug's return to Lauren. She deserved a nice surprise, too.

When she opened the door, concern lined her face.

"Is Connie getting worse?"

"I don't know. Maybe not." She glanced over her shoulder to where Brian and Connie sat at the kitchen table. "I can't be sure."

"Let's see if we can get her mind off it," he suggested. "They always say if you can distract them from the pain, it's not real labor."

"What do you know about real labor?" she teased.

"Not much, really." He raised his voice and smiled at Connie and Brian. "But I do know a lot about Monopoly. I was the Forrester Farms' champion."

They played until Connie finally stood. "I'm going to go to bed and try to get some rest." She ruffled Brian's hair. "You about ready to turn in, sport?"

"Sure. Good night, Miss Lauren. Night, Mr. Jeff." The boy hugged them both and bounded down the hall to the guest room, where Lauren had made up a cot for Brian.

"Thank you, both, for everything you've done," Connie said and followed her son.

"What did she mean? Did you tell her about the roof?" Jeff whispered when she was out of sight.

Lauren shook her head. "I think she meant caring for them in general. They've not had a lot of that in their lives."

"No, I don't guess they have. But I have a feeling things are going to take a turn for the better for them."

"Oh, really?" Lauren punched his shoulder. "Now you're telling the future? Is there anything you can't do?"

"Trust people. Apparently I have a real problem with that."

Her smile faded. "We're going to have to work on that."

He thought of his bargain with Doug Miller. "Believe

me, I am." With a flick of his wrist, he tossed the empty food cartons in the trash. "Do you know it's only three days until Christmas Eve?"

She gave him an inquisitive look. "You read minds, too? I was just thinking about that."

"They're counting on me to bring you home, you know."

"Jeff, there's no way I can leave Connie and Brian all alone with the baby coming. Or even if it comes before then, they'll still need help."

Not if they have Doug to take care of them. "We'll wait and see what God has planned. How about that?"

She wiped off the table. "I guess. But don't get your hopes up about me going back with you. I'm not going to leave them to fend for themselves."

"Gotcha. How do you feel about leaving them alone for a few minutes right now and slipping out to look at Christmas lights with me?"

A huge smile wiped all the worry from her face. "Oh, Jeff, that sounds like something I can do."

When they exited the interstate at a suburb Lauren recommended, they could see the lights. Every house was trimmed with sparkling lights, and the lawns were decked out like the North Pole.

"Want to walk?" Jeff asked. He and Lauren shared a love of the outdoors.

"Sure."

He parked, and they ambled slowly down the street, taking in the intricate details of each display. "Even though they're all sort of alike, they're each one different," Lauren said softly. "Kind of like people."

Jeff pointed out a wobbly-legged reindeer with a bright red nose and hummed the first few bars of the familiar tune. Lauren grinned and broke into song. He joined in, and when they couldn't remember the reindeers' names, they made them up, until they were both laughing so hard they could hardly walk. "Sonnet? And Blondie?" He raised an eyebrow and looped his arm through hers. "Lauren Forrester, you just flunked Christmas 101."

"Right. You've got a lot of room to talk. Splasher and Stupid were definitely not pulling the sleigh."

"It's been a long time since we used to watch those TV Christmas specials when we were kids."

"For your information, I've never missed a year. I even watched them with Brian this year."

"I can't believe I didn't know that!" He knew she

loved Christmas, but he had never dreamed she still watched the old TV specials.

"There's a lot about me you don't know." She punched him on the arm and took off to the truck at a dead run. By the time he caught up with her, she was in the passenger seat laughing.

Lauren snuggled deeper into the patio chair with her down comforter tucked tightly under her chin and stared out at the city lights. The vastness of the city made her feel so small. A stereo played Christmas carols in the distance, reminding her of home. Loneliness welled up inside her. She was a friend to many, a good friend to a few, best friend to one; but when push came to shove, she was alone. Ever since Jeff had started his quest for the perfect girl, she'd felt their bond slipping through her fingers like buttered toffee.

She rested her head back against the frame of the chair and looked up at the dark sky. It wasn't like her to indulge in a pity party, but surely being away from home for the holidays gave her the right for a short poor-me session. Jeff would have a fit if he knew she stayed out on her patio at night. Someone might scale the building and grab her, he'd say. He was so protective. Sometimes she fooled herself into thinking that meant he cared about her as more than a friend; then she'd remember that her brothers were protective, too.

She'd almost let her guard down tonight when they were looking at the Christmas lights. As soon as she'd told him there was a lot about her he didn't know, she'd realized her mistake. Jeff would hound her until he figured out what she meant. So she'd hit him and run. Maybe it wasn't the most mature decision, but it was definitely the most expedient.

There had been a glint in his eye, though. And as she was running, it had flitted through her mind that if this were an old movie, she would let him catch her. When his arms were around her, he'd realize his deep love for her and kiss her passionately. If this were a movie, of course.

An unfamiliar sound pulled her from her cinematic fantasy. She clutched the comforter and hurried back into the apartment. Jeff's cell phone lay on the dining table playing a tune. Without even stopping to think, she snatched it up. "Hello?"

"Is Jeff there?" a female voice sobbed. For a split second, Lauren wondered if she'd fallen asleep on the balcony and was dreaming. This sudden drama seemed like a scene out of a movie.

"No, no, he's not. He left his phone—"

"This is Krista." Her words were barely recognizable.

"Krista, it's Lauren. Are you okay?"

"Oh. Hey, Lauren." She seemed to calm down some. "I'm sorry. I just need to talk to Jeffie. Would you ask him to call me?"

"I'll tell him tomorrow." Lauren realized Krista had broken the connection.

She sank down at the table, her heart pounding in her throat. How childish she'd been to think Jeff had come to St. Louis because deep down he loved her and didn't realize it. He'd probably just been restless, smarting from a fight with Krista, and decided to tool on over to see his buddy for a while. Too bad for him that he'd left his phone on her table or everything would be patched up by now. Krista obviously wanted to work things out. And Jeff? Krista was his perfect woman. What more could he ask for?

Lauren locked the patio door and unplugged her

tabletop Christmas tree. Bah humbug. As she shuffled into her bedroom, her gaze fell on the picture by her bed—she and Jeff on the Ferris wheel at the county fair. They'd been seventeen and had the world at their feet in more ways than one. She picked up the picture and flung herself back across the mattress. How had she let her life get into such a mess?

A tap sounded on her open door. She looked up to see Connie standing in the doorway. "You asleep?"

"No." Lauren pushed to a sitting position on the edge of the bed, then looked down at the framed photo she still held in her hands and blushed. "Just thinking about what might have been." She motioned to the armchair across from her. "Come on in."

Connie waddled into the room, her arms resting on the top of her enormous abdomen. She looked at the picture as Lauren placed it back on the bedside table. "He's a great guy."

"Yep. The best friend a girl could ever have," Lauren said.

Connie lowered herself gingerly into the chair. "The connection between you two seems to go deeper than friends."

"Only on one side, I'm afraid." Lauren felt her grin tremble.

"Don't give up on him yet." Connie shook her head. "I thought Doug and I were through, but now that we're both Christians—I've never loved him more. And I know he feels the same way."

"Jeff doesn't see me like that. Never will. To him, I'll always be good old Lauren." She reached out to touch the picture one more time, then looked at her new friend. "But I'm going to stop obsessing over that and get on with my life. When Doug gets out and you and Brian"—she smiled at Connie's stomach—"and the baby are taken care of, I'm going to move home."

"Oh, Lauren, I'm so glad." Connie clapped her hands together softly. "The city is in my blood, and I love it here, but it's no good when you're only here because you're running away from something. You belong in the country. It's your home."

Lauren jumped up and hugged Connie. They embraced for a few seconds without speaking, then Connie took her hand. "I'll never forget what you've done for me, Lauren. God used you to take care of us. I'm so grateful that you were here."

"Even if I was running away?" She grinned.

"Proof positive that God can use anything for good."

"Touché."

Later, as she drifted off to sleep, she thought about Connie's words. God really had used Lauren's impulsive decision for good. And Jeff's presence had been for the best, too, since it had gotten Connie's roof fixed. And Lauren wasn't sure it was the handiwork of God, but she knew it was for the best that Jeff had left his phone there. If not for the phone call from Krista, Lauren might still be imagining what would have happened if she'd let him catch her.

Chapter 7

Push me that bundle of shingles, will you?" Jeff glanced over his shoulder.

Doug slid the package across the roof. "You're pretty fast at this."

"Years of experience. I've been doing carpenter work since I was in high school."

"That's how I am with cars." Doug cleared his throat. "But I'm not bad with a hammer. There's no excuse for the shape the house is in."

"You were out of town," Jeff said, surprising himself by wanting to make the man feel better.

"Don't kid yourself. This disrepair didn't happen in

eight months. It was the drugs. They took my life, and I let them."

"Like my mom. Except she could never see it. Right up until that final fatal overdose, she'd denied using drugs. Then it was too late."

"Overdose?" Doug asked quietly.

He nodded. "She was dead when I went in to tell her I was leaving for school." He sat back on the roof, hammer hanging loose in his hand. "My grandparents took me in and raised me. Still, it always rankled me that my mom didn't care more about me than she did the drugs."

Doug scooted over beside him. "Ah, man, that's rough. Since I didn't know your mom, I can't say for her personally, but I can tell you that I loved Brian and Connie more than the drugs. But the drugs. . ." He picked up a roofing nail and flipped it around in his fingers. "They captured me. I was a slave to them. It was have them or die. Even after I got clean, I didn't have freedom. Not until Rick introduced me to Jesus."

"Mom knew about Jesus, but I don't think she really knew Him." Jeff thought back again to all the times they'd milked the local churches for charity. "There were times when she was sober that I thought she loved me, though. I wish she'd made different choices."

"That's a lot for a kid to handle. So that's why you're willing to help people like me get a second chance. I appreciate you fixing our roof more than you know."

Jeff felt his face grow hot at the undeserved praise. "We'd better get back to work if we're going to finish this today." He hammered one shingle on after another, but his heart was hammering, as well, as he thought about what Doug said. Why hadn't he tried to help others? Deep down, he'd believed people like Doug were getting what they deserved. How could he not have realized that if he wanted God's grace he had to share it with others?

He prayed as he hammered, and by midafternoon, he'd started the journey toward forgiving his mother. His heart was considerably lighter. "I think that about finishes it up here, Doug."

"It looks great. Thanks again, man." Doug gathered up an armload of tools and carried them down the ladder.

Jeff picked up what was left and followed him. As they packed the things in his truck, he smiled. "I have to go over to Lauren's and get my cell phone. You want to go with me and bring your family home?"

"I can't think of anything I'd like better. Seems like I've been waiting a lifetime for this moment. I think I'll change into a clean shirt, though." He paused with the front door half open and looked back at Jeff. "Want to see the inside? I've been working on it at night, trying to make everything like it used to be, only better."

"Let me close this up and I'll be right in."

Doug had just disappeared into the house when Lauren's little blue car pulled up to the curb. She and Brian got out and ran up the sidewalk.

"Jeff, Connie's in labor."

He looked behind her. "Is she with you?"

"She's at the hospital. They said it would be a while before anything happened, so we ran over to tell you." She held up his phone. "Since we couldn't call you."

"Thanks." He slid the phone into his pocket.

Brian had moved away from them and was staring up at his newly repaired roof, eyes shining.

"I wondered if you'd come stay with Brian at the hospital," Lauren said softly. "I don't want to leave Connie alone."

Jeff grinned. Some days were made for surprises.

"I will, but there's someone else who will want to come along, too."

"Really?" Lauren's brows knitted together. "To the hospital?"

The front door of the house opened, and Doug walked out, buttoning the top button on his shirt. He saw Brian and stopped, mouth open.

"Dad!" Brian threw himself at his father, and Doug picked him up and spun him around.

"In the flesh."

"I can't believe you're here!" The boy stood in the shelter of the man's arms. They showed no sign of separating.

Tears streamed down Lauren's face as she looked at them and then back to Jeff. "How did. . . ? Did you know?" She shook her head and laughed through the tears. "Are you behind this, Jeff Warren?"

"Not me, Laur. This is all God's doing." He blinked against the prickly moisture in his own eyes. "Let's go let Connie in on the surprise."

"We named her Lauren," Connie said, her voice still a little weak.

Lauren stared through the blur of tears at the little bundle of pink in her arms. "I'm honored. It meant a lot to me to be here to welcome her into the world." She'd tried to excuse herself, but Doug and Connie had both insisted she stay in the birthing room with them. Jeff had kept Brian occupied in the waiting area.

"We couldn't have done it without you," Doug said from his perch on the edge of Connie's bed.

"We sure couldn't have," Connie echoed. "Does holding her make you want one of your own?"

Lauren looked down at her namesake again. How could she explain that she'd had an earth-shattering, plan-destroying revelation during the past few hours? She knew now, beyond a shadow of a doubt, that this was what she wanted. What Doug and Connie had, in spite of their difficulties. And yes, children, to love and nurture. She couldn't speak for the lump in her throat, so she just nodded and gently jostled the baby.

Connie and Doug continued to chat, but their voices faded to a muted roar in Lauren's ears as she put her finger in the baby's palm and watched her little fingers curl around it. How could she ever have considered staying single and childless? If God had planned that for her, she'd live with it, but how could she consciously choose it? She'd been crazy to think she could move home and be satisfied with her old job and Jeff's friendship. She'd never find someone else in the shadow of his presence.

"Lauren, are you okay?" Connie's voice jolted her from her thoughts.

Lauren nodded and walked over to the bed. "She's so beautiful."

"You won't get any argument out of us." Doug's thin face seemed to radiate light. He reached out his arms, and Lauren carefully placed the baby in them.

"I'm going to go let Brian come back in, okay?"

"You'll be back, right?" Connie asked.

Lauren forced a big smile. "You can't get rid of me that easy, girl. Aunt Lauren is here to stay."

They all laughed, but Lauren saw a twinge of concern in Connie's eyes.

She walked slowly out to the waiting area. "Brian, your folks thought you might want to come in and stay with them." She looked over his head at Jeff. "Want me to run you to get your truck?" They'd all been in such a hurry to get there that they'd piled into Lauren's car together. As much as she dreaded being alone with him, she knew he needed his truck.

"That would be great." He walked over and put his arm around her. "You worn out?"

She relaxed for a minute against him, then pushed herself upright. "A little, but nothing like Connie, of course."

"The baby's something else. Did they tell you her name?" He grinned at her as they walked through the parking garage.

"Yeah. I couldn't believe it."

"I wasn't really surprised," Jeff said as he slid into the passenger seat. "You made a huge difference in their lives."

"I didn't do anything special."

Lauren reached for the stick shift between the seats, but Jeff captured her hand in his. "Everything you do is special," he said softly. The cold interior of the car seemed to shrink and warm up as she felt his thumb caress her hand. His face was so close to hers, she could see his breath. "Home is not the same without you, Laur. Won't you at least go back with me for Christmas?"

He was right there, his eyes so blue, his mouth so chiseled and appealing. Lauren wondered if he could hear her heart pounding. If she leaned one inch toward him. . .

A loud ringing filled the small car. They both jumped, and he plucked his cell phone from his pocket. He glanced at the caller ID, then dropped it again without answering it.

Lauren put the car into gear and maneuvered out of the parking garage. "Was that Krista?" she asked, hoping her tone was casual.

"Yeah, but I'll get in touch with her later."

Lauren kept her eyes on the road. "She called last night after you left your phone at the house. I meant to tell you, but then Connie went into labor." She willed her eyes not to water. It had been an emotional twenty-four hours. "Krista sounded pretty upset."

"She's having a rough time."

Then why don't you hightail it home and make up with her? Put all three of us out of our misery? Lauren bit back the snippy questions, but in her heart she knew with certainty that she'd be spending Christmas in the city.

Chapter 8

"Want to go shopping?" Jeff asked, smiling when Lauren whipped her head around to give him an incredulous look.

"Shopping?" she repeated as if her hearing must be bad. "As in at the mall?"

"Yes." The way he figured it, here was a chance to kill two birds with one stone. Lauren was obviously feeling blue about something, and that precious little baby was going to need some clothes and nursery items. So the mall was the obvious cure for both problems. "I thought we might get baby Lauren a few things, then take them back to the house and set it up for when they bring her home tomorrow."

Her eyes sparkled, and she swung the car in a wide U-turn. "That sounds like a marvelous idea. I can't believe you thought of it."

He laughed. "Do you think I'm so dumb I don't know that was an insult?"

"I never said anything about you being dumb," she said, concentrating hard on the road.

One objective down. She was cheering up already.

When they got to the mall, Lauren insisted they forgo the toy store for the clothes department. "She doesn't need a life-sized giraffe, Jeff. Her life will be enough of a zoo if you're ever around."

"It's not my fault you're always making a monkey out of me," he shot back. "But you're probably right. We should start with clothes. Then we'll hit the toys."

Jeff tucked his arm in Lauren's as they walked through the mall, but she jerked it away. "Got to keep my muscles in shape for carrying bags," she explained, flexing her arm.

Right. When did she get to where she couldn't stand for him to touch her? He didn't say anything, though. Assuming she went back home with him, they'd hash it out after Christmas.

Two hours later, they had enough baby clothes to last for a while. "What about nursery furniture?" Jeff asked.

"Connie has all of Brian's at the house. It might need to be cleaned up a little."

"Is that next on our to-do list?"

"Sounds good to me," she said, wandering over to a store window.

He followed her and stared up at the dress in the window. "That would look great on you."

"Not me, silly. Connie. I want to get them each a little something."

"Me, too. But not enough that they will feel obligated to get me something in return." He cleared his throat. "Actually, they've given me enough already."

She looked at his reflection. "What do you mean?"

"Talking to Doug made me face some truths about my mom. She was a flawed person, just like the rest of us, Lauren."

She stepped back against him, and he rested his head on the top of her head and lightly put his arms around her. Their reflection stared back at him in the shop window. To his amazement, they looked like—a couple. The idea shook him, and he barely heard her next words.

"I'm glad you got to know Doug and talk to him about things."

Jeff forced his thoughts away from how good it felt to hold her and back to their conversation. "Me, too. I've thought of Mom as a monster so long that I didn't realize how much that anger wore me down."

She turned, still in his arms, and for just a second leaned against him. He grinned. He'd always teased her about smelling like citrus fruit, but as the aroma of tangerines floated up to him, he realized how much he'd missed that scent. He pulled her closer and felt her stiffen. She pushed back, brown eyes wide, face pink. "I'm really happy for you, Jeff." She ducked out of his embrace and hurried into the store. He stared after her. What had gotten into her? For that matter, what had gotten into him?

Lauren arranged the zoo animal mobile over the crib and stood back. She and Jeff had compromised. He'd gotten his giraffe, but miniaturized.

She and Jeff had a blast gathering things for the baby and gifts for the rest of the Millers. They'd worked at the house last night, then met here this morning to do some last-minute things before going to the hospital to get Doug, Connie, Brian, and the baby. She'd invited Brian to stay all night at her house, but he'd wanted to be with his parents, and she didn't blame him.

She and Jeff had talked on the phone until late. It had been like old times. They'd talked about her missing Christmas Eve at Granny's and about him forgiving his mom. About everything. Except her feelings for him. And his feelings for Krista. They neither one mentioned her.

Lauren thought of all the awkward times yesterday when she'd pulled away from his touch. He probably thought she was crazy. Which in a way she was. Crazy about him.

She still saw the irony in the fact that she'd left home to get away from him and he'd followed her. Especially considering he did it based strictly on platonic feelings. What would it be like to have Jeff, in love with her, come charging into town to beg her to come home? She wouldn't last ten minutes.

"You ready?"

She looked up from where she was fussing with the crib dust ruffle. "When you are."

"That's an old stalling trick. Means you're not quite ready."

"Is that what it means?" She ran her hand over the balloon wall hanging and edged toward the door. "Beat you to the car!" She threw the words back over her shoulder and took off for the living room.

"Oh no you don't." He caught her before she made it halfway down the hall and started to tickle her.

"We have to go," she choked out and slipped from his grasp, then hurried to the front door. She should have seen that coming. If he got out of town without her giving her feelings away, it would be barely short of a miracle. "Should we take my car so there will be room for everyone?" she asked, willing her voice not to tremble.

"Sure." His voice was subdued, and he hardly looked her way as they got into the vehicle.

The silence hung in the air between them as they drove to the hospital, but the Millers were so exuberant about going home that Lauren found it hard not to be excited with them.

The afternoon flew by as Jeff and Doug and Brian

worked together to make everything perfect for an astonished Connie, who had assumed they were going to Lauren's apartment. After several trips to the nearby pharmacy and grocery store, the house was as well-stocked as Lauren had hoped. She put on a big pot of chili and threw some grilled cheese sandwiches together while Connie and the baby rested.

After supper, Jeff pushed to his feet. "I'm going to have to go."

Lauren raised an eyebrow. "Home?" She frowned when she heard her voice squeak.

Connie excused herself with the baby, and Doug and Brian followed close behind.

Like rats deserting a ship, Lauren thought. *Just when I needed them most.* The last thing she wanted was to be alone with Jeff while she was trying to be strong.

"Yep. I checked out of the hotel this morning." He stood there in the kitchen and stared at her. "I'll wait for you to get your stuff together if you want to go. If you don't want to drive, I can bring you back whenever you're ready."

She shook her head and swallowed hard. "I appreciate it, Jeff, but I think I'm better off here this year."

"If I could make one iota of sense out of that, I sure would be happier," he said. "But I reckon it's your business." His blue eyes darkened.

She forced herself to remain seated between the wall and the table.

"You sure you won't reconsider?"

"I'm sure." She looked down at the faded plastic tablecloth and picked at an imaginary speck. Why didn't he just go? If she stood up to tell him bye, she'd run out to the truck as hard as her legs would carry her.

"Merry Christmas, Lauren."

She gave him a little wave. "Merry Christmas to you, too."

And then he was gone. And so was her heart.

When the door closed behind him, she put her head down on the table and let the tears fall.

Chapter 9

The snowflakes swirled at Jeff's truck windshield faster than the wipers could dispel them. If it were daylight, the snow would, no doubt, be beautiful, but as Jeff drove down the dark interstate, it surrounded him like an oppressive white blanket. Along with freezing temperatures and the starless night sky, the never-ending barrage of snowflakes fit perfectly with his mood.

Even though Lauren had repeatedly told him she wasn't coming home for Christmas, he'd never really envisioned himself making this return trip alone. In tandem maybe, paving the way in his truck as she followed close behind in her little blue car. He'd call her occasionally to make sure she was making it okay, and they'd stop at the halfway point and get a drink or a bite to eat.

But in the end, he'd left her behind. She hadn't even really given him a proper good-bye, although he wasn't sure anymore what would have constituted a proper good-bye from her. More than the wave of her hand he'd gotten, that much he knew.

He was grateful God was helping him work things out as far as his bitterness toward his mother. But Lauren. She unsettled him. Their friendship didn't fit anymore. It was like a pair of boots he'd loved but outgrown. It pinched his heart and made it uncomfortable.

He'd almost kissed her in the car yesterday. The realization shook him to the core. He would have if his phone hadn't rung. Assuming she'd have let him. She'd seemed agreeable to the idea, but maybe that was his imagination. Ever since that moment, things had been out of sync between them. She was avoiding him. He'd tried to play around and even started to tickle her while they were over at Connie and Doug's house getting things ready for them to bring the baby home, but she'd slipped from his grasp without a giggle.

As he remembered how she'd been in his embrace one moment and gone the next, he gripped the steering wheel and fixed his eyes on the snowy highway. Familiar scenery greeted him now, but he felt like he was getting farther and farther from home.

"Lauren? Are you going to stand there and watch the snow fall all night?" Connie called.

Lauren turned away from the window. "Did you see how the flakes are coming down sideways? The wind, I guess." She walked over to the worn orange and brown plaid couch where Connie cradled the baby in her arms and sat down beside her. "I'm just glad we're going to have a white Christmas."

"Hard to believe tomorrow's Christmas Eve, isn't it?" Doug asked from his seat on the rug next to Brian. They'd dragged out an old Lego set and were trying to outdo each other with their elaborate creations.

"Yeah." Lauren sighed. It would be the first Christmas Eve morning she'd ever missed eating breakfast at Granny's and hanging ornaments on the tree with her cousins.

"You seem thrilled about it." Connie shifted the baby to her shoulder and patted her gently on the back. "Tell me again why you're not going home."

"Connie, I'm afraid to. This thing with Jeff. It's gotten too big for me to keep it a secret. And I really don't want to spend the holidays making an idiot out of myself over someone who views me as a good buddy." She grimaced and fiddled with the baby's little crocheted bootie. "Plus, I've got to make a clean break if I'm ever going to meet someone else."

Connie motioned toward Brian and Doug, who were absorbed in building their Lego structures, then waved a hand at the rest of the modest house. "Who are you hoping to meet here, girl?"

"It's too soon to be thinking about that, really," Lauren said, fully aware of how ridiculous she sounded.

Connie raised an eyebrow at her. "Do you ever really listen to yourself?"

"What do you mean by that?"

"You are the oddest mixture, Lauren Forrester. You forced Brian to bring me to the library that day to talk to you and then insisted we move into your apartment. I'd never met anyone so straightforward. Yet you won't tell this man—this man that you've known since forever—that you're in love with him and take a chance that he might feel the same way."

"What about Krista?"

"What about her? From what you've told me, you don't know that he has any feelings for her at all, only that she called him crying." She motioned toward the muted TV with her free hand. "If I called the star of that TV show crying, would that mean he was in love with me?"

Lauren ran a finger down the soft skin on the baby's neck. "Your mama should be a lawyer, little Lauren."

"That's what I tell her all the time," Doug said.

Connie's face turned red. "I'm looking into getting a grant for college. We'll see after baby Lauren gets a little older." She turned back to Lauren. "If I can consider going to law school, you can surely march yourself down to your granny's and tell Jeff how you really feel. Give him a chance to tell you he feels the same."

"You never give up, do you?"

"Not if I think there's any hope of success."

Lauren pushed to her feet. "Anybody want a cup of hot chocolate?"

"Sounds wonderful," Connie said. "You're not going to poison me because I'm telling you like it is, are you?"

Lauren laughed. "I don't think I have the nerve to do what you're saying. Risk a lifetime of friendship on a chance of love."

"Are you happy being just friends?"

"No."

"Then I don't see where the risk is."

Lauren ambled into the small kitchen and fixed four cups of hot chocolate. She craved the comfort of chocolate. And if she were honest, anything to get her mind off of tomorrow and off the fact that Jeff was gone.

As she was setting the cups onto a wicker tray, her cell phone jangled. She snatched it up. Had Jeff decided to stay in town? To ask her one more time to go home with him? "Hello?"

"Lauren? It's Krista."

Lauren's heart thudded against her ribs. "Hi, Krista. How are you?"

"I'm okay." The girl laughed softly. "I got your phone number from Jeff. I hope you don't mind."

"Oh. That's fine."

"I felt bad about being so upset on the phone the

other night. I just wanted to say I'm sorry—and to tell you my good news."

"What good news?" Lauren's legs suddenly felt like jelly, and she sank onto a bar stool.

"I'm engaged."

"Oh." Tears filled Lauren's eyes, but she forced herself to speak. "Congratulations."

"It's mostly because of Jeff."

Of course it is, Lauren thought, head spinning. She clutched the phone like a lifeline, even though she wanted to throw it down and stomp on it. "Really?"

"Yes, he helped me to understand how Ron was feeling."

"Ron?" Lauren felt like someone had switched channels in the middle of a show. She shook her head to clear it.

"We had a big spat the other night," Krista continued as if Lauren hadn't spoken. "That's why I called Jeff, to get his take on it. But it's all worked out now. Ron was going to give me my ring back for a Christmas present, but he couldn't wait. So tonight he asked me to marry him."

"Krista, I'm so happy for you." Lauren meant every

word, but she still wasn't sure exactly how this had all happened. "Are you going to Indiana right away?"

The girl laughed. "I'm in Indiana! Didn't Jeff tell you? He advised me not to stay away from Ron another minute, so I took all my vacation time two weeks before Christmas and came home."

"Oh, that's good." Lauren tried not to growl, but why hadn't Jeff told her that? At least that miscomprehension wouldn't have stood between her and telling him the truth.

"Everyone should be home at Christmas. When are you leaving for Pierce City?"

"I'm heading out first thing in the morning."

She heard a cough and looked up to see a beaming Connie standing in the doorway giving her the thumbs-up sign. "Good night, Krista. Congratulations again. Thank you for calling." When she pushed END, Connie started laughing.

"Krista's engaged, huh?"

"Yep." Lauren sat at the table, still trying to take in the news.

"And not to Jeff?"

"No."

"So is it possible, Miss Forrester," Connie said in her best lawyer voice, "that if you were mistaken about that detail, you could also be wrong about Mr. Warren's feelings or alleged lack of feelings for you?"

"I don't know," Lauren said, smiling. "But tomorrow I intend to find out."

Chapter 10

At 1:00 a.m. Jeff gave up on sleep, got dressed, and peered out his living room window. The snow had stopped, so he padded out to the old swing set. He kicked the snow off the swing and sank down to lay his confusion down at the feet of the One who could make sense of it. As he finished praying, a figure tromped toward him from Lauren's parents' yard. The man drew closer, and he recognized Lauren's dad, a big overcoat thrown over a white T-shirt and black sweatpants tucked into his snow boots.

"Jeff? You okay?" Concern filled Mr. Forrester's voice.

"Yes, sir. I'm all right. Just couldn't sleep."

"Me, either. I was getting a drink and saw you out the window. Thought I'd come out and keep you company. Hope you don't mind." The older man perched in the other swing and almost lost his balance. He chuckled. "Truth is, I miss my little girl."

Jeff took a deep breath. "Truth is, that's my problem, too, sir."

"You two have been close for a long time." Mr. Forrester gave Jeff a sideways glance. "It's bound to be hard not to be together at Christmas."

Jeff had to stand up if he was going to say what he had to say. He pushed out of the swing and walked over in front of the man. "There's more to it than that. At least there is on my part. I don't know how she feels because I haven't told her yet, but I'm in love with her." He felt like all the breath had been pushed out of his lungs. The long ago conversation with his grandfather about "us" and "them" played over and over in his mind. He rushed on. "I'd like to ask your permission—"

The swing set shook as Mr. Forrester jumped to his feet. "You don't know how proud I am to hear that!" He grabbed Jeff's hand and shook it. "I thought you were never gonna wake up, boy."

"I—I—I. . ." Jeff wanted to tell him that Lauren probably didn't love him back, so there was really nothing to shake his hand about, but Mr. Forrester pulled him into a hug.

"I guess you know we've always loved you like a son."

A lump the size of the Ozarks filled Jeff's throat. "I love you and Mrs. Forrester, too. You've all been really good to me over the years."

"So when's the wedding?"

"I'm going to drive to St. Louis in the morning, but I can't guarantee anything." What a difference a few minutes could make. He'd been certain that Lauren's dad wouldn't think he was good enough for his daughter. "I might go back right now."

"Take some advice from an old man," Mr. Forrester said. "No woman wants to be proposed to while she's still got morning breath and no makeup. Get a good night's rest and give her time to miss you. You show up around noon tomorrow, and she'll be tickled to death to see you."

Jeff remembered how casual Lauren had been when

they'd said good-bye. He was probably setting himself up for heartbreak, but what would his life be like if he didn't try? He shook Mr. Forrester's hand one more time and forced himself to go to bed. When sleep came, he dreamed he was on one knee proposing to Lauren. She had the baby's little zoo mobile in her hand, and she was shaking the monkey in his face and laughing. Finally, he fell into a sound sleep and didn't wake until morning. The snow had started falling again.

He prayed as he dressed in his least-faded jeans and blue and green flannel shirt. Just before he walked out the door, Granny Forrester called.

"Jeff?"

"Good morning, Granny." He'd been surprised by Mr. Forrester's proclamation of love last night, but he'd never doubted that Granny loved him like he was one of her own grandkids. "What's going on?"

"That's what I want to know. You got in from St. Louis last night?"

"Yes, ma'am, but I'm heading back there this morning."

"Whatever for?"

"This is just between you and me, so if you talk

to her on the phone before I get there, you can't say anything—"

"I won't say a word. What's the big secret?"

"I'm in love with Lauren and I want to—"

"Whoo-eeee!"

He held the phone away from his ear. *Like mother, like son,* he thought, remembering Mr. Forrester's premature celebration. "Now, wait a minute, Granny."

"Stop by here before you go, Jeff."

"I'm running late—"

"I won't hold you up. See you in a few minutes."

"Yes, ma'am."

Five minutes later, he stood on the snow-covered porch of the big, old, white house and rang the doorbell. No one answered, so he pushed the button again. Finally, he heard running on the steps and the door flew open.

His heart flip-flopped. Staring back at him, her gorgeous brown eyes wide with surprise, was Lauren.

"Jeff? What are you doing here?" Lauren cringed as she realized how that sounded. She'd spent the whole trip from St. Louis this morning gathering her nerve, but she'd also promised herself a leisurely breakfast and a confidence-building girl talk with her cousins before she confronted Jeff about her feelings. Yet here he stood, on the doorstep, as breathtakingly handsome as she'd ever seen him.

"Granny called and asked me to come by. I was on my way to—what are *you* doing here?"

"Why don't you come in and I'll explain?" She stepped back for him to enter, then closed the door behind him. Forget the confidence building; it looked like it was now or never.

When they were settled on the sofa, Jeff touched the fresh greenery that laced between Granny's snow globe collection on the coffee table in front of them. "Granny didn't cut back on her decorating this year, I see."

Lauren shook her head. "If anything, I think she added a few things." Her mouth felt as dry as the inside of the Santa birdhouse gourd that sat on the table across from her. "I'm actually glad you're here."

"You are?" Jeff reached over and took her hand gently in his.

She resisted the urge to pull away. She was done running.

"I'm glad you're here, too." He kept his gaze on her thumb as he caressed her hand absently with his thumb. "Saved me a trip back to the city."

"Why were you going back to the city?"

He looked up at her then, and she saw stark fear in his eyes, but unless she was crazy, there was something else behind the fear. Suddenly she knew. He loved her. "Lauren, I need to tell you something. And if you don't feel the same way, I hope we can still be friends."

"I thought I was the one who talked too much. If you don't hurry up, I'm going to have to tell you first." She looked down at their hands, completely intertwined now. Their hearts had always known the truth; it was just taking their brains a little while to catch up.

"Tell me what first?" He stared at her. "Lauren? Are you saying you love me?"

"Of course I do. Why do you think I ran halfway across the state to get away from you?"

"I tried to get you not to go." He grinned, and a glint of mischief sparkled in his eye. "Anyway, I guess you know it's your fault I never did find my perfect girl, you know."

"It was not. I even memorized your list." She jerked her hand from his and began to count off the qualities on her fingers. "Good with kids. Blond—"

"See? That explains it. It was always brunette. I just hated for you to know that you were pretty much my idea of the perfect girl."

"Pretty much? What do you mean pretty much?" Lauren couldn't believe how free she felt. Her best friend was back, only better than ever, because he— "Wait a minute. You still haven't told me you loved me."

"You know what your Granny always says."

"Never go out in the cold with your hair wet?" Lauren gave him a cheeky grin, but her heart thudded against her ribs.

"No, silly. Actions speak louder than words." He leaned toward her and whispered, "I love you," then lowered his mouth to hers. For a while no words were needed.

CHRISTINE LYNXWILER

Christine thanks God daily for the joyous life she shares with her husband and two daughters. They work, play, and worship together in a small town nestled in the gorgeous Ozark Mountains. She loves to write and has had several novels and novellas published with Barbour Publishing.

Joy comes from many corners, and at this point in her life, Christine's list of blessings include a wonderful husband and two amazing daughters, a large family (including in-laws) who love God and each other, a close group of writer friends, a loving congregation of believers at Ward Street Church of Christ, and readers like you who encourage and support her dream of being a writer. Please visit her Web site at www.christinelynxwiler.com and sign the guestbook to let her know you stopped by!